Saved By a Soldier

Love Conquers Life, Book 1

By Alison Mello

Saved By a Soldier

LIMITLESS PUBLISHING

Limitless Publishing, LLC
Kailua, HI 96734
www.limitlesspublishing.com

Formatting: Limitless Publishing

ISBN-13: 978-1-68058-664-0
ISBN-10: 1-68058-664-5

Dedication

There is a story behind this book and I'd like to take a second to tell it. One morning I got a private message on Facebook from this woman, Patty. She was inviting me to join a book group called Bonded By Books, and at first I was quite leery. When I found out she was a friend of my friend Lynne and that Lynne had invited me, I decided to join. It turned out to be one of the best decisions of my life. Patty and the rest of the ladies in this group are amazing. Thanks to this group I have made some pretty special friends. My writing journey began with this wonderful group of people who supported me and encouraged me.

This book started out like any other in my book world until one morning I woke up and discovered a fundraiser was taking place to raise money for Patty. She had been diagnosed with cancer and we all wanted to do what we could to help her. I decided to donate the main character in my next book to the silent auction that was taking place. The winning bidder would get to name the main female character in my book. Well, Terri See bid on my auction item and won. When Terri messaged me and asked me if I would write the book for Patty I was honored and admittedly a bit nervous, wanting to write something as special as she is.

Patty, my friend, this book is for you. I hope you enjoy reading it as much as I've enjoyed writing it. You're a special person with a heart of gold. Your strength during a tough time in your life is a true inspiration to us all. I wish you many more years of happiness and good health.

Thank you, Patty, for inviting me into this special group. Without you I may not have started writing and therefore have the opportunity to write this book for you.

Chapter 1

Patty

"Joan, I know you want the next book submitted in a few months. I'm just having a hard time getting it on paper, but I'm working on it." I roll my eyes because she's totally freaking out and I don't know what her problem is. I've yet to let her down.

She yells into my ear, "I want to see the first five chapters by the end of the month."

"You're giving me three and a half weeks to write five chapters? Do you realize some authors take a month to write one chapter?" I say, pacing my living room.

She sighs into the phone. "Listen, it doesn't have to be perfect, but I need to see you're working on it. Pull your head out of your ass and get to it. Go away somewhere if you have to, but I want to see some writing from you and soon."

I roll my eyes in frustration. "You do realize this pressure makes it harder for me to write, don't you? But have no fear, I'll see if I can get my dad's lake house for a few weeks. Who knows? Maybe I'll find some inspiration up there."

"Patricia, you know I love you, but my boss is freaking out because I told her you were taking time off." She calms down and sweetens her voice. It's totally fake and pisses me off. "You have had some time, now I need to do my job and I need you to do yours. Get me a book please."

"Joan, how many books have I written for you?" I say tersely.

"Five, two of which are still on the bestseller's list."

"Great. So go tell your boss I'm working on it and I'll talk to you in a few weeks. I have to go so I can find out if the house at the lake is available and get some stuff together to move out there for the next few weeks."

I end the call totally frustrated. I can't believe that she is pressuring me like this. I published my last book about six months ago, so I don't know what her rush is. I warned her I was taking a break after the last one. Apparently she feels my break is over. I haven't taken any time for myself since I first started writing about two years ago and I really needed this break. I shake my head, five books in two years. There are top authors who take a year to write and perfect one book.

I started writing for Joan straight out of college. I graduated as an English major with a dream of publishing a bestseller. I knew the easiest way to get to the bestseller's list was to hire an agent. As soon as my first book was written I started submitting to as many agents as I could. The agency Joan works for was willing to take a chance on me. My first three books did well but my last two really took off and got my name out there.

I plop myself down on my couch to call my dad. I put my feet up on the coffee table and take a deep breath, then dial his number. "Hey, Daddy," I say when he answers my call.

"Hey, pumpkin, what's going on?"

"Daddy, I need to use the lake house for a few weeks so I can focus on writing. My agent is driving me crazy and if I don't show her some work soon, she's threatening to drop me."

"I'm not sure I like the idea of you being out there alone for an extended period of time, pumpkin. Let me see if anyone is at my buddy Jackson's house so I can have someone keep an eye on you."

"Daddy, I'll be fine. I just need some quiet and the lake is a perfect place for that. Plus it's beautiful out there so I'm hoping to find some inspiration."

"All right, pumpkin, it's all yours. Please let me know once you're out there though."

"Okay, Daddy. Well I've got to go because I need to pack so I can get there and start working."

I cut the call and head straight to my room so I can get to it. I'm piling clothes on my bed as I think about my next book. I've had the basic idea for a while now, but for some reason I can't seem to turn it into a book. While I'm thinking about it, I make a mental note to grab my notebook with all my random thoughts. Every time I have an idea for a book I jot it down on whatever I can find and then add it to this notebook. Then when I'm ready to write I pull out the notebook to look over what I've got. This notebook has gotten me through five books.

I groan as my mind wanders back to my frustration with Joan. Don't get me wrong, I'm proud of my work and I love what I do, but the last two making the bestseller list has my agent up my ass for more and I hate being pressured.

As I go through a mental checklist, I realize I need to call my bestie so she won't freak out when she doesn't hear from me for a short period of time. Her phone rings and she answers with a groan.

"Hello?"

"Did someone have a rough night?" I respond with laughter.

"You have no idea. What's up, Patty?"

All my close friends call me Patty. To be honest, I don't have many because I was never the popular girl in school. I was more of a book nerd who cared more about my grades than being popular. A lot of the friends I do have are on Facebook and I've made some through book clubs and writing. Bella and I have been best friends forever. She's the only one who ever stood by me when everyone else was picking on me for being that book nerd.

"Just wanted to let you know I am heading to my dad's lake house to get some writing done. I wanted to give you a heads up so you wouldn't worry."

"Is that bitchy agent of yours on your ass again?" she says, suddenly more awake.

I chuckle. "Yeah, something like that."

"I thought you were taking some time off. You need some time for you. You haven't had a relationship since dickhead and you need a man in your life."

"Bella," I groan. "I do not need a man in my life. I need to write so my agent doesn't drop my ass for lack of work. Besides no one wants my scrawny ass anyway." I mumble the last part not really wanting her to hear me, but of course she does. I'm now staring at myself in the mirror looking up and down my body. I'm tall and ridiculously thin with boring brown hair and small B cup boobs. I can eat anything I want and never gain a pound. I know some girls would love a body like mine, but personally I think I'm a bit too thin.

Bella brings me back to our conversation yelling into the phone. "Patty!"

"What?"

"You need to stop! You're gorgeous and any woman would kill for a figure like yours."

"I know. I guess I just wish I had a little more meat on my bones and I need to find time to do something about this hair. I have to get a new headshot taken and you know how I feel about pictures."

"When you get back we'll do a spa day together. You can get your hair done and then have your picture taken afterwards. Let me know when you're scheduled to be back in town."

"I will. I have to run because I really need to finish packing and get my car loaded up. I still have to stop and buy food for the lake house after I drop off my stuff."

"Call me and keep me posted."

"I will, Bella. Bye." I cut the call and get back to

packing.

Bella makes me laugh because she is gorgeous with beautiful blonde hair and the brightest blue eyes. She can have any man she wants, but she's picky as hell. I'm glad she won't settle though, because some of the guys she's dated have been complete asses and just want her for her body and her money. No matter how much I have always doubted myself, she has done everything she can to make me see the best in me.

It's getting chilly here and it will be worse at the lake so I grab a few sweaters and long sleeve shirts, as well as jeans and a few pairs of my favorite yoga pants.

I finish packing my clothes and am bringing my stuff to my living room when my phone rings. It's my mom. I roll my eyes and think *Did he really call my mom?* My parents divorced when I was small and they hardly ever talk, so I don't understand why he has to call her now. I split my time between two homes growing up. Both my parents had money but my mom has always been a bit snobby and flaunts her money. She tries to make me dress and act like her, but I'm really all my dad. I think that's why they ended up divorced. My dad may have money but he doesn't show off like my mom does.

"Hello, Mother," I say as I head to the other room to grab my laptop, notebook, and anything else I may need for writing this book. I'm wrapping up the charger to my phone and laptop when my mother starts in with her whining.

"Patricia, my angel, your father tells me you are going to stay at that awful lake house of his," she whines. "Please let me put you up in one of my hotel suites. You'll be so much more comfortable, darling, and it's much safer there."

"Mother, I like the lake house. It's quiet and has a beautiful view, that's what I need."

"Fine, then I'll book you in a beautiful room abroad somewhere, just name the place."

"Mother, that's just not necessary. Let me get through this next book and then you and I can take a trip together somewhere if you'd like. I'm not going to sit in another country somewhere to write my book when I can do it a couple of hours from home."

She pauses while trying to figure out what to say next. I know it's because she's been defeated. I can hear the cogs in her head turning as she's contemplating her next move.

"Fine, Patricia, if that's really where you want to write. Just please be careful and call me so I don't worry about you."

I know she cares about me but we want different things in life, and although she tries to support me, she also tries to push me toward her lifestyle. My ex, who Bella loves to refer to as dickhead, was a set up by my mom. He's rich as hell but treated me like complete shit. My mom thinks I should have dealt with it so I can stop working and I'd be set for life. I say screw that. I'd rather be broke and in love then be set and treated like shit.

"Thanks, Mom. I love you."

"I love you too, dear."

I gather the last few things I need and head out the door toward the lake house.

***

The ride out to the lake has been a breeze. There's next to no traffic and the scenery as I drive down the highway is absolutely beautiful. I arrive in about two hours to find it just the way I remember it. The lake house is a gorgeous gray and rock home with a farmer's porch that stretches the length of the house. It's fall here so the leaves have all turned beautiful shades of yellow, orange, and deep red. Tons of leaves are covering the ground and my dad's old boat is still sitting by the dock. I step out of the car taking a deep breath of the clean, crisp air. I reach into the car to grab one of my bags and as I walk to the door I look around, thinking about some of the great memories I have coming here as a child with my father. My favorite swing is still here hanging from the ceiling of the porch. I think about all the time Bella and I sat here just hanging out, creating some of my fondest childhood memories. I take one more deep breath to enjoy the clean air before I step into what I'm assuming will be a stale house. I'm not sure how long it's been since my father was last out here, so it may be a bit musty inside.

I unlock the door and step inside, utterly shocked because the place is spotless and it smells delicious in here. There's definitely some sort of home cooked meal being made.

"Hello?" I call out, wondering if my father forgot he let someone else use the house.

"Hello, Miss Patricia." My mother has sent Celia, her housekeeper, to take care of me.

"Hello, Celia. How are you?" I ask as I walk over and give her a hug.

I adore Celia. She has been around since my parents divorced when I was a little girl. She's getting older now and over the years we have become quite close. She has always understood that I'm not my mother but my own person, and I need to live my life for me. We've had many talks growing up about the simple fact that my mother means well and just wants to see me happy.

"I'm well, Miss Patricia. I want you to know that I understand you wanted to be alone here and I promise to not get in your way. Your mother was going to come out here and I thought it would be best if I volunteered instead."

"Thank you, Celia. I appreciate that."

"It's no problem. Is there anything I can do to help you get settled?"

"No, I'm going to grab a few more things from my car and I'll be right back. Is that lunch you're making?"

She gives me a warm smile. "It is and it'll be done shortly, so go get settled."

I go back out to the car, shaking my head at my mother's constant interference in my life. She just doesn't get it. I can take care of myself. Collecting the remainder of my things I go back in and head straight to my room. When I walk in, Celia is there putting fresh linens on my bed.

"Thanks, Celia. I could've done that."

"It's no trouble, Miss Patricia. I enjoy taking care of you."

"Please call me Patricia or Patty when mother

9

isn't around."

She simply nods and exits the room since she's done with her task. I grab my phone to call my mom as I continue to put my things away. I really hate living out of suitcases and need some sense of order in my life. "Hello, Mother, I just got to the lake house."

"I'm glad you made it saf—"

"Mother, you didn't need to send Celia, but thank you."

"I worry about you when you are in 'writing mode,' as you call it. You don't eat very well and I want to make sure you're taken care of."

"I would've been fine, but again thank you I appreciate the thought. I'm going to go, because lunch is almost ready and I have a few more things to put away."

"All right, darling, I'll call you to check in soon."

"Goodbye, Mother."

As I'm putting my last item away my stomach grumbles, and that's when I hear Celia calling to telling me that lunch is ready. I head into the bathroom to wash my hands before going to the kitchen to eat.

She places a bowl of homemade chicken orzo soup in front of me with my favorite grilled ham and cheese. I give her a huge smile. "You're the best."

She winks at me. "You're welcome," she says before she leaves me to my lunch.

I take a bite and moan in appreciation. Celia's a wonderful cook and she makes me things I like and not the stuffy dishes my mom likes. I take my last bite and head to the sink to clean out my bowl and plate, placing them in the strainer to dry. I decide I need to go for a walk so I can clear my head and think about the book I'm working on. I started this book once but I just wasn't feeling it, so I've decided to start over again.

"Celia, I'm going for a walk to clear my head. I'll be back shortly."

Chapter 2

Carter

"Come on, Dad. You have got to be kidding me."

"No, Carter, I'm not. All you do is sit around this house all day sulking anyway. I know you have been through a lot but it's time for you to pull your life together. This is a good chance for you to clear your head and figure out your next steps in life."

My father stands over me while I lounge on the couch. I jump up into a sitting position.

"Babysitting some snotty brat while she writes a book is not exactly what I had in mind for my next step in life."

"I understand that, son, and I'm glad that's not your plan." He sits on the side of me. "I was hoping for more from you." He slaps me on the knee. "Besides she's not a snotty brat, her mother is a snotty brat. She is more like Troy, and I owe him. You know he brings in tons of money to my banks with his dealerships, so please do me this favor. All you have to do is go hang at the lake and keep an eye out to make sure she stays safe. You don't even have to talk to her or interact with her. As a matter of fact she's not even supposed to know you're there."

I growl because I'm pissed that I'm even considering this. I don't know this woman but I know her mother. She's a tall blonde with nice blue eyes and most guys drool over her, but her snotty attitude makes her ugly in my opinion. She's such a bitch. I had the luxury of meeting her at an event I was attending with my parents a few years ago. It was a huge fundraiser and she snubbed me because I was *only* a soldier. I shake my head.

"Fine, Dad. I'll go, but you're going to owe me. I just spent the last two years in and out of the desert babysitting teenagers who didn't know their ass from their elbow and now I'm going to sit at the lake to babysit again."

He starts laughing at me. "You act like my lake house doesn't have heat and running hot water. It's well-kept and has all the amenities. Hell, you even have internet and cell service out there."

"Well I guess I better get packing." I leave our living room to get a few things together.

"I'll have the cleaning service go out to freshen it up and stock it with food for you while you get your stuff ready. Just remember she doesn't know you're there to watch out for her. She's going to think you are just staying at the house."

"I got it, Dad!" I yell from my room, annoyed. He acts like this is my first mission. I'm thirty years old and I'm going to babysit. My father asked me because he knows the soldier in me will not allow any harm to come to this woman. He knows I'll protect her at all costs because it's what I do. Or should I say, what I *did*.

I'm not home because I want to be, I'm home because of a stupid knee injury that cost me my career. I guess I'll use this time to weigh my options and maybe even start applying for some jobs. I debate with myself because one moment I have all the motivation in the world and the next, I am sitting around and doing nothing, which sounds really good.

I pull my duffle bag out from under the bed and throw a bunch of clothes into the bag, not even paying attention to what I'm taking. I know I have jeans, t-shirts, sweatshirts, a little bit of everything. I fit as much as I can into it then toss my shower kit on top and head back out into the living room.

"What, no shave before this mission?" my father says, busting my balls.

"Real funny, Dad." I scratch at the rough beard that is starting to grow on my face. I hate having facial hair but I haven't had much of an urge to shave either. Come to think of it, my hair is way overgrown too. I guess I really do have to get my shit together, though I have no desire to do that either. I've only been home a few months, and I have done nothing in that time. After all I saw on my last tour, I needed some time to clear my head of all the horror I experienced.

I grab the keys to my Jeep. "I'm out of here. I'll call you once I get there and have eyes on the princess," I call out over my shoulder as I leave.

Dad laughs. "Okay, son. Drive safely, and thanks."

I throw my bag in the back of my Jeep and jump in the front seat. I start the car and crank up my music, heading first for the local coffee shop before I hit the highway. It's about a two hour drive to the lake and since I haven't been sleeping well, the caffeine will do me some good.

I'm cruising along the highway when my cell phone rings. I answer it on speaker through my Bluetooth system. "Hello"

"Hey, Carter. What's up man?"

"Jordan! What's going on?"

"Nothing, what are you up to this weekend?"

"Dude, get this. My father needs me to head out to the lake to watch over his buddy's daughter. She's a writer or something and is hiding out at the lake to get some work done. Daddy is worried about his little girl." I roll my eyes.

"Oh man, that kind of sucks, but maybe she'll be smoking hot. You know you haven't hooked up in a while."

"If she's like her mother, she'll be a total snobby bitch and that alone will make her ugly. I can't stand that shit."

"Whatever. When will you be back in town so we can hang?"

"I don't know. I need to find a job though."

"I told you I can get you a job in construction with me."

"Dude, you work crazy hours and I'm a soldier not a carpenter. That's all you."

"Whatever, man. Just hit me up when you get

15

back. We need to plan a guy's night out."

"Will do!"

I cut the call and my music instantly starts blaring again. Jordan's cool but his parties are too much for me. I'm the calm one who would rather just chill at home than hang in a bar or club.

I pull up to the lake house, where a cleaning crew is there going through the entire house. I walk in, drop my bag, and tell them that I'll head to the store to get supplies while they're finishing up.

"There's no need. Your father had us stock the place, so you're all set," a guy with a vacuum on his back tells me.

I plop myself on the couch wondering what the hell I'm going to do with myself over the next few weeks. I know one thing is for sure, I need to start working out again. I haven't lifted, run, or practiced my martial arts since I've been home. It makes me wonder if my weights and equipment are still in the spare room. I head down the hall and there they are. It makes me smile, and that's something I haven't done much of lately. I change into some workout clothes, and then grab my phone and my docking station so I can have some music playing while I work out.

I go at it hard for the next hour thinking about nothing but what I want to do with my life. Since I'm a veteran, I can probably land just about any job I want, but I want to do something that'll make a difference. I want to find something that I'll enjoy doing. I don't want to just get up and go to work every day for the sake of filling time or so I can say I have a job.

Once I'm done with my workout, I decide to take a shower and then check out things around the property. I get some clean clothes and my shower kit and as I head to the bathroom, I realize the cleaning crew is gone. I drop off my things in the bathroom then head to the kitchen to see what they stocked for me. I open the cabinets and laugh because there's nothing that I can even cook in here. There is only juice, milk, and soda in the fridge. I chuckle as I pick up my phone to call my father.

"Carter, please tell me you didn't just get there."

"Nah, the cleaning crew was here. I decided to hit my workout room while they finished so I wasn't in the way."

"Oh good. Bet it felt good to work out again, huh?"

"Yeah, somewhat."

He's been hounding me to get back at it and I'm not ready to admit he was right.

I sigh. "Um, did you tell your cleaning crew what to stock for food?"

"Not really, why?"

"Dad, you know I can't cook and they left me stupid stuff. Make sure you don't pay them for much on the food. I'm heading to the store to get some supplies and some beer. I won't be gone long. If you need me just call my cell."

"Okay, son, thanks again."

I disconnect the call and walk off to take a shower before I run to the store.

As I drive into town, I'm hoping I don't see anyone that I know. People in this town are nosey and they all know I served and that I'm home on medical discharge. My family and I spent a lot of time here while I was growing up. My father liked coming out here even after I had outgrown the place and he couldn't wait to brag about how I was joining the Army, proudly telling everyone I was going to serve my country. Although I was quite proud and I still am, I don't like to talk about it. People only want to hear about the glory, they don't want to hear about all the gruesome details of what really happens. As far as I'm concerned, it was a career choice and I was just doing my job.

I pull up outside the local store. It isn't very big but has everything I need to get me through my stay here. The lake house my father bought is kind of in the middle of nowhere. There's one gas station, one store, and a few small shops. A lot of the roads are narrow and some are even dirt. There are only two houses on this side of the lake. My dad owns one and his buddy Troy owns the other. The opposite side of the large lake is a bit more crowded and a bit further from the shops, but some of them house residents year around so it keeps things going here.

I walk into the small store and find the owner, Mr. Silver, behind the counter.

"Is that Carter Montgomery I see walking into my store?" he shouts with a big smile.

I head straight over to him. I smile and shake his hand. "Hi, Mr. Silver. How's it going?"

"I'm doing swell, son. How are you?"

"I'm doing okay. Hanging out at my dad's for a few weeks while I figure out what I'll do with myself now that I am home."

"If you get bored and you want something to do

stop in here. I'm sure I can give you some work. It won't be much but at least you won't just be sitting around."

"Thanks, Mr. Silver. I'll keep that in mind. For now I think I can use some downtime."

"I can understand that. Go get what you need."

Being a war vet himself he's one of the few people who understand what I went through and that I don't want to talk about it.

I head off toward the aisles to search for what I need. I get some beer and water to keep in the fridge. I need to stay hydrated if I'm going to be working out, and I enjoy a beer with dinner. I like to eat healthy but it is hard when you can't cook. I collect some cold cuts, wheat bread, veggies, and fruit, plus some simple canned soups and stuff that I can just heat up. God I wish my mom taught me how to cook.

***

When I'm pulling up to the house, I see a woman wandering around outside and I know it must be her. I sit in the car watching her for a second. She's really too simple to be the daughter of Sandra Fitzgerald. She's wearing a pair of jeans that have tears in the front with a red turtleneck and a long sweater that she has wrapped tightly around her thin body. I'm stunned. She's simple but pretty at the same time. Her gorgeous long hair flows in waves down her back and although she has this pained, lost look on her face, she's beautiful.

I climb out of my jeep with the bags in my hands

19

and mosey into the house, nearly walking into a tree because I'm so distracted. I shake it off and hurry inside before she sees me. I'm supposed to be discreet, and already I feel like I'm failing miserably.

Chapter 3

Patty

"Celia! I'm back!" I shout as I walk in the front door.

"Did you have a nice walk?" she asks, walking into the living room.

"I did. Do you know anything about the man staying in Mr. Montgomery's house?"

"No. Why?" I can tell she is just as surprised as I am.

"First, I am surprised Dad called my mother to tell her I was staying here. Now there is a guy staying next door and he just happens to arrive the same day I do. I can't help but feel like he set that up too."

"I walked into the room as your parents were finishing their conversation and when I asked if everything was okay your mother told me that your father was concerned about you staying out here alone. Your mother started to push the idea of her coming. I thought it would be better for me to be here, which is why I volunteered."

"Thank you for that. Clearly my parents don't listen to me. I'm going to the den now to do some work."

I walk away with my laptop bag in hand and sit down at the desk. While my laptop is booting up I pull out my notebook and a pen. I have some notes written on the story and where it will go. Now I just have to start piecing it together. I rearrange my thoughts on paper so that I have some ideas on when I want certain things to happen in the book.

Opening my laptop I click on the Word icon to open a blank document and begin typing. I've never been a writer who maps out their book fully before they start. I've always been able to simply sit down and write. The first two chapters or so can be difficult, but once I get going I can usually keep my book flowing without a problem. For some reason, this book has been the toughest to get started and I think it's because I feel like I have to top the last book. My agent is putting too much pressure on me and that really makes it difficult to produce good work. During my walk today, I decided to clear my head of all that is my agent and my last book. My only thoughts are of what I want my story to be and I'm simply going to write it, she'll get it when I'm ready.

I'm writing about a lonely woman who is nearly thirty and has yet to experience love. She has dated but ended up either hurt badly or met men who couldn't keep her interest. That is, until she finally meets 'Mr. Right.' The problem is she's now so full of doubt she can't see that the man of her dreams is right there in front of her.

Having the gist of the story is the easy part. It's creating all of the details while keeping my readers interested that's the problem. However, a few hours later, I manage to have the first two chapters completely written and I'm quite proud of myself. I decide to rub it in my agent's face by sending her a text.

Patty: Chapter 1 and 2 written more to follow.

Joan: Nice! Are you at the lake?

Patty: Yes. I need to do some posting online now so I can get my followers thinking about this next book. Talk to you later.

Joan: Talk to you later.

I open my Facebook author page and write:

`Guess who has started their next book? Yup, me! Who's excited to see what comes next from the world of P.A. Fitzgerald?`

I click post and in a few minutes' time I have followers responding, stating how excited they are about my next book. I also go onto my web page and add the book to the work in progress section of my website with a brief idea of what the book will be about. I've started getting quite a few hits on my website so I want to make sure I keep it up to date. I also add a brief blog entry letting my readers know that I'm still around but hiding out writing my latest book.

Now that I'm done with my posting, I click on my notes icon and read through what I have. My agent is trying to get me to write a trilogy but I'm just not sure I have it in me to write three books about the same couple. That takes a bit more planning, but she keeps telling me it would be the next best romance since *Fifty Shades of Grey* and *The Crossfire Series*. Despite telling her that I have no desire to be compared to either of those trilogies, I've been putting some thoughts on paper in case I change my mind. Although I will not allow myself to be compared to them, I will be the best me I can be and that is it.

One issue I have always had as a reader is waiting years between books to see what happens next. As a writer, I would have to feel like I had enough in mind to write all three books close together so my readers are not waiting forever to find out what happens next. Looking at my notes I am not anywhere near there. I'm adding ideas all the time and my notes are growing but I'm still not ready, so Joan's going to have to accept the standalones I send her for now.

There's a knock on my office door, and I look up I find Celia standing there. "Sorry to bother you Patricia, but dinner is ready. Would you like me to leave a plate for you or are you ready for a break?"

I smile, welcoming the break. "You have perfect timing. I'll be right there."

"Great." She leaves the office to finish preparing our dinner. I close my laptop and head to the bathroom so I can wash up for dinner. When I reach the kitchen I see she has already set a plate out for me.

"The house smells delicious, Celia."

She has made baked chicken with mashed sweet potatoes and green beans. My stomach growls, telling me I'm hungrier than I realized.

"Thank you. Do you mind if I join you?"

"Are you kidding? I was hoping you would, Celia. I really didn't want to be out here all alone. It would be so lonely and boring but I really needed to get some work done. If I had brought Bella or my mom with me I'd get nothing done."

"I understand." She laughs lightly. "So how have you been? I feel like it has been forever since I've seen you."

"I know. I'm sorry but if I go by to visit mother, then I have to pretend to be someone I'm not and it drives me crazy. Visiting her is hard, that's why I don't come often. I wish she would just accept me for who I am."

"Your mother loves you very much," Celia says with a sigh. "She just wants the best for you. Although I totally understand what you're saying, please just try to remember that."

"Oh I know, that's how I ended up with that asshole Ben. He was the worst boyfriend ever, but because he has money she insisted he was perfect for me. She said he could take care of me." I shake my head, remembering all I went through with my ex. I stayed with him for over a year trying to please her and hoping that he would change and we could have a normal relationship. But when he hit me, that was it, and I was out the door. My mother actually stood up for him, saying he didn't mean it and that he had too much to drink that night. I didn't want to hear it. I was done.

Celia gives me a sympathetic look and takes another bite of our delicious dinner.

"Listen, I know you're loyal to my mother and it's fine that you don't want to say much. You have told me enough times how you feel and I know you're there for me."

"Thank you, Patricia. I care a great deal about you and your mother. I truly believe your mother has your best interests at heart. It just isn't what you want, and that's fine too. Continue to show her who you are and what you can accomplish and she'll come around." We continue to eat in a comfortable silence until Celia says, "What's up with the boy at the Montgomery house?"

"What do you mean?"

She smiles. "Was he cute?"

I burst out laughing, "Celia, I hardly saw him. He ran inside like he was afraid to be seen. All I know is he had some grocery bags in his hands like he was going to be here for a while."

"Maybe he'll provide you with some inspiration." She wiggles her eyebrows up and down and I blush.

"I bet this is my father's doing. He probably sent him out here to watch over me. My mom sends me an awesome cook and a buddy and my father sends me a knight in shining armor."

Celia chuckles.

"This was delicious," I say as I stand to scrape

my plate and wash it.

"I'm glad you enjoyed it," Celia says, drying the dishes I'm washing. It's then that I realize how lucky I am to have her with me. It's nice to have someone to talk to during meals and to help make sure I'm eating well.

"Thanks for being here, Celia. I mean it. I know we only just got here and I complained about wanting to be alone, but it was nice to have someone to have dinner with." I hand her the last dish to dry off.

"I'm glad to be here, Patricia. If I had let your mother come, you wouldn't get anything done and you would probably kill her."

We both start laughing again.

"I think I'm going to go take a bath and relax in my room for a bit. Good night, Celia."

"I have some white wine in the fridge if you would like to relax with some after your bath. I'll be lighting a fire."

"That sounds nice, thank you. I think I'll grab a book and do just that. Give me about twenty minutes and I'll be out."

I head into the bathroom deciding to shower instead of bathing so I can sit down and read. I have quite the collection of romance books and I read a variety of subgenres. I tend to stay away from the darker reads, though. Some of them are too creepy for me, but I'll read just about anything else. I jump in the shower with the intention of washing quickly so I can get to my book, but the hot water feels so good it slows me a bit. I finally get out ready to get back to the erotica read I'm in the middle of.

When I get back to the living room, the fire is burning and there is a chilled glass of wine sitting on the coffee table waiting for me. I smile at just how good Celia is to me. I bet she has already gone to bed so I can have some time to myself. I love the living room here. It isn't large, but that's what makes it so perfect. The couch is close enough to the fireplace to make it cozy. I can feel the warmth from it without being too hot and there is a slight aroma of burning wood. I love the smell. I love to look into the fire and watch the flames dance. I think it is so pretty and relaxing.

I pull the coffee table a little closer to the couch so I can reach my wine easily and snuggle up in a blanket by the fire. I take a few sips and I moan in appreciation as I enjoy a glass of my favorite Moscato.

As soon as I start to read my phone buzzes. It's Bella texting me, I see from the display.

Bella: *How's the writing going?*

Patty: *Two chapters done and shoved in my agents face :-P*

Bella: *LOL you are the best, so when will you be back?*

Patty: *Hopefully in a few weeks. My mom sent Celia out here so I'm not alone. You should plan to come and visit this weekend.*

Bella: *I'll be there! How about I come down*

Saturday afternoon?

Patty: Sounds good to me, see you then.

I pick up my book and start to read again. It's a great story, but not something I could ever write. I'm not afraid to write about sex, but I can't write the nitty gritty that is in this book. This is the *Fifty Shades of Grey* stuff that my agent wants, very detailed and explicit. As I lay here reading it, I start to think that Bella may be right. I am getting lonely. I have not been with a man in over a year and I'm tired of going through Battery Operated Boyfriends. I swear I should have stock options at the local sex store. One of the girls even knows my name. How embarrassing is that?

Chapter 4

Carter

I wake with a headache and since I only had a few beers I know I'm not hungover. I must be dehydrated from working out. I groan when I realize I may not have any aspirin. I rise from my warm bed wearing nothing but boxers and head to the kitchen for some water. I might as well stop there first because the hard-on I'm rocking will certainly make it difficult to piss. I chug the entire bottle, grab a second, and wander into the bathroom. I check the medicine cabinet and to my surprise it's fully stocked. I down two aspirin and start the shower. Despite the fact that I feel like shit, I want to work out again today so I can start trying to develop a new routine.

Once the water is warm, I step in. I lather my hands with soap and start stroking my fully erect cock. I'm still hard as a rock from the wonderful dream I was having about little miss writer next door. I imagine her sporting a school girl outfit with my hands in her hair as she takes my cock in her mouth. I start fucking it until she's practically gagging on my length. In a matter of minutes, I'm pumping every last drop of cum down the drain. I sigh because that gave me some relief but it really isn't what I want. I haven't slept with a girl in god knows how long, and if I don't get to bury myself balls deep in some pussy soon, I think my dick is going to fall off.

I shut the water off, not bothering to wash the remainder of my body because I'm only going to get sweaty working out and will shower again in a bit. After putting on some gym clothes, I head to the kitchen to start a pot of coffee, so it will be ready when I'm done with my workout. You would think after years of shitty coffee in the Army I would be over my caffeine fix, but I still need coffee to start my day.

To start my workout I jump on the elliptical, jamming with music going for thirty straight minutes. I like my elliptical because it's as close as I can get to running without actually running. Next I move onto lifting for the next thirty minutes and then practice my martial arts, panting from how out of shape I am. I grab my towel when I hear my phone buzzes and I see it's my dad.

Dad: There's a job opening at the local VA office

Carter: Sweet, I will go online and look at it.

Dad: My buddy said he's pretty sure he can get

31

you the job if you apply.

Carter: Nice. Getting in the shower now and then I'll apply.

I set my phone down and smile, genuinely excited about this opportunity. That's a job that I think I would really like doing. I would get to help soldiers who have been discharged both honorably and medically get the benefits they deserve. I actually may be getting my life in order. I was feeling like I was screwed when I got shot in the knee. When they told me that they needed bolts and screws to repair it, I knew my career was over. I had knee replacement surgery and they don't let you stay in the Army with a bunch of nuts and bolts in your leg.

I take a second to stretch. I can already feel my body stiffening since I haven't been working out and I hit it hard yesterday too. I jump in the shower and wash quickly because I want to get on my laptop to apply for this job. I can feel my knee getting sore, which means I either overdid it or rain is coming. I look outside and sure enough, the rain is here. Despite the fact that rain puts me in pain, I enjoy it because it calms me. As a kid, my dad and I would sit on the porch of this house watching the rain bounce off the lake. It's one of my greatest memories. We would spend hours upon hours talking about life, sports, or whatever other conversation came up while we sat there and rocked.

After I get dressed I grab my laptop, coffee, and

cell phone and head out to the porch. I send a text off to my dad.

Carter: Sitting on the porch watching it rain while I fill out the application.

Dad: Nice, just like old times huh.

Carter: Yeah, only this time I have no one to talk to.

Dad: Do you need me to come down?

Carter: Nah, I'm good, but thanks Dad. I'll talk to you later.

Dad: Talk to you later son.

I take in a deep breath of the clean, crisp air, open the web browser, and go to the site my dad told me about. The first posting available is the one I'm interested in. I click "apply" so I can start uploading all of my information. I didn't even read the description because to be honest, it would be an honor to work for the VA. I don't care what the job is, and I know my dad would never steer me wrong.

It only takes me a few minutes to upload the required information and my resume. I look up when I hear the door open next door. I see the woman from yesterday walking out of her house to sit on her porch with a cup of coffee just as I am. So much for being discreet. I'm trying so hard to not look in her direction but it's hard because our houses are not that far apart and there's something about her. I pretend to busy myself on my laptop so I'm not staring, but really I am. I notice she has a notebook or sketch pad in hand and it appears she's taking notes, but she looks up to the lake every once in a while. I think I even catch her looking in my direction, but I can't be sure. She's probably wondering who I am and why I'm here.

I can't believe with our fathers being friends, and all the time I've spent up here, I've never met this girl. Shit, I don't even know her name. Now I'm pissed that I didn't think to ask my father. I try to distract myself by logging onto my social media so I can see what's going on. I was hoping to find Jordan online so we can make plans to hit a club or something in a few weeks. That typically isn't my scene, but I haven't been out in so long I need to do something to try and meet a girl.

I jump when I hear her burst into laughter and that's when I notice how beautiful her smile really is. She has the most perfect white teeth I have ever seen. They're so bright and perfectly straight and those full luscious lips. I dreamt about them around my cock last night, which is how I woke up with a hard-on. I can't help but stare at her and when she busts me I just give her a brief smile before I look back down at my laptop. I already have email from my father's friend asking me if I can come in for an interview next Friday. I send an instant response saying absolutely, and ask for a time. He responds back telling me that he'll see me at three. I'm happy to have an interview, but I realize that I don't know if princess will still be here. I better send my father a text.

> *Carter: Hey dad! I have an interview next Friday at three.*
>
> *Dad: That is great!*
>
> *Carter: Yeah but if princess is still here she won't have a babysitter.*
>
> *Dad: Please stop calling her that. Her name is Patricia and I'm hoping she will be back. Her mother has a fundraising event next weekend and I know her mother's going to try to get her to go.*
>
> *Carter: Ok*

Feeling like someone is watching me I look up and she's staring at me with a slight grin on her beautiful face. I chuckle and look back down at my laptop. So, the princess has a name. Patricia. I can't imagine a girl like that would want to be with a messed up guy like me.

I flash back to the day that ended it all for me. There is screaming all around me, bullets flying, and all I can think about is getting to Brody. I can hear him screaming my name. I run toward him, and my knee buckles. I hit the ground hard, jump back up, and keep running to him. When I reach him, I collapse to the ground by his side in pain. Brody is really bad off. I shake my head, trying to wipe away the horrible memories of that day. Not only did my career end but I also lost one of my best friends. It's a day I will never forget.

Patty

"Celia, I'm taking my coffee to the porch."

I want to sit and watch the rain while I think about what I'll write next. I've always enjoyed watching the rain, my mom says it's boring but I think it's relaxing. As I get comfy with my coffee and notebook, I see that guy is sitting on Mr. Montgomery's porch. He must be his son because he looks somewhat like him. I quickly look down to my notes since I don't want to be caught staring.

The air smells of fall rain and it is so relaxing. I can hear the rain hitting the water and I love the sound it makes. I come up with an idea for the next chapter of my book so I jot down some notes. One of the lines I have written makes me burst out into laughter. I do that all the time, laugh or smile at the things I write. My hand flies to my mouth as I stop myself, embarrassed that he's now looking at me. I've probably interrupted his morning and I'm sure he's now thinking, *what's that crazy lady up to?* I try to pretend like he's not there watching me but it is hard. I can feel his eyes on me and I can't help but look. He's really attractive and I find I'm having a hard time looking away. It's like we are looking into one another's eyes, connecting even though we know nothing about each other. His hair is overgrown and he needs a shave, but I like the messy look he has going right now. He looks like he is pretty well built too.

I give him a smile and a slight nod. I feel a slight blush creep up as I bite my lip. I look back down at my notes, breaking whatever connection we just had. I'm really thinking more about him than I am my book. When I peek back up, he is looking down at his laptop with a pained look on his face. He looks like he's reliving something or in deep thought. His brows are furrowed and his eyes are closed. It makes me wonder what's worrying that handsome man. Feeling like I'm invading some sort of private moment I look back down at my notebook.

Maybe I should introduce myself to him. Wait, what if he doesn't want to be bothered? What would he care to talk to a lonely bookworm like me? When I look back up to give him a smile hoping he'll walk over here, he's typing on his laptop again and it makes me feel like I missed my chance. I sigh and go back to my work.

A short time later I'm out of coffee. I glance over one more time. He's gone inside. I go in too, make myself another cup of coffee, and send a text to Bella.

Patty: There is a hottie staying in the house next to me.

Bella: No way, did you introduce yourself?

Patty: Ummm, No! Why would I?

Bella: Maybe because you're single and you

deserve a man in your life.

Patty: Trust me he is not the type of guy who dates shy bookworms like me.

Bella: Ooohh girl, wait until I get there, you need to see you are gorgeous and not a bookworm.

Patty: Whatever, I'm going to write so I can take Saturday and Sunday off. Talk to you later.

Bella: Later.

I walk into the office with my coffee and notebook and settle in for a few hours of writing. I open my laptop to start with reading what I wrote yesterday. I always start with that because I end up finding mistakes or making changes that make the story better. It seems I notice things better after I've taken a break. Once I have finished and I'm satisfied with what I have written, I pick up where I left off yesterday. I'm having a hard time focusing though. I keep thinking about my neighbor's handsome face and the look of pain it held.

I really need to dig into my work, so I push all thoughts of him to the back of my head. I don't want to be stressed when Bella gets here this weekend. I'm partway into chapter three when I hear a knock on the door.

"I brought you a sandwich and some chips for lunch."

"Thank you, Celia. I was so busy I hadn't even

realized it was lunch time yet."

"Not to worry. I didn't want to interrupt you, so I brought you something you could eat in here."

"Thanks, you're the best. Oh and by the way, Bella is coming up Saturday afternoon. If I know her she will be here by Saturday, late morning."

"That's great! I will plan to have her for lunch and dinner on Saturday."

"She is spending the night so she will be here for breakfast and possibly lunch on Sunday too."

"Okay good to know. I'll run to the store to pick up you ladies some wine and munchies for your girls night as well as something special for dinner."

"Thanks, Celia."

While I eat I'm going to do some posting in my online groups to take a break. Maybe that'll help me clear my head so I can focus on my writing more. I love my groups and have made a lot of friends over the years. I post in one of the groups that I'm back to writing and my friend instantly replies.

Marissa: What happened to the break?

Patty: It's over

Marissa: That was a short break

Patty: Too short, but you know how it is, the readers want more.

Marissa: The readers? Or your agent wants more.

I laugh at this comment because she publishes traditionally without an agent and she tried to convince me to stay away from agents, but I didn't listen. She says she has more control over her career, and she's probably right, but oh well.

Patty: A little of one and more of the other, I will let you decide which is which.

Marissa: LOL, drop that agent of yours. You would have no problem getting published without her.

Patty: I'll think about it ;-)

My agent may be a bit of bitch but she has done a lot for me, so I don't really want to bash her. I just need to make it clear that a break means, like, a year, and that's what I will be taking soon.

Chapter 5

Patty

It's Saturday morning and I'm pretty excited that Bella's coming up to visit today. I've been hard at it and have sent my agent another chapter. I told her I was partway into the fourth in the hopes that she'll relax a bit. Bella is a lot of fun, but she won't let me even think about my book or my agent while she's with me. Sometimes I wish I were as strong and confident as she is.

Bella is a model for one of the top agencies in the area and has had many contract deals. My mom has often said things like, 'I wish you would dress more like Bella.' I'm thankful my best friend understands that I'm not her and I don't want to dress like her. I have no need to wear expensive, uncomfortable clothes when I work from home. The only time I have to dress nice is when I'm meeting with my agent. I dress a little nicer for her, although it isn't too much of a step up from my normal jeggings and a tunic with a messy bun.

41

Bella is a gorgeous tall blonde with crystal blue eyes and a stunning body. She only wears the top brands because if she is caught out somewhere dressed in anything but, the press has a field day. The thing I love about Bella is that she isn't bitchy or snobby. She loves everyone for who they are and doesn't think she's better than you because she's a model and wears great clothes.

There's a knock at the door before it opens. "I'm here!" she shouts, walking into the lake house.

She has spent so much time here with us over the years it's like her home too. Bella may have money but she wasn't born with it. She and I have been best friends for years, actually we're more like sisters. Her parents were kind of shitty and stopped talking to her when she made modeling her career and so my parents stepped up to support her in her journey. I don't understand why her parents were so against it because she's very successful and has done well with it.

"Bella!" I run and hug my best friend. "I feel like it has been forever since we've hung out."

"I know. I'm sorry, Patty, my schedule has been crazy lately between gigs and parties with networking. It's what I do. The good news is things are slowing a bit so I'll have a little more time to hang out."

"That's great and I don't want you to feel bad. You're awesome and you look amazing as usual."

"I brought you something."

"What?"

"Your mom is part of a huge fundraising party next weekend, as I'm sure you know, and she's really hoping you will attend. I thought if I brought us dresses that coordinated, you would be more open to going with me."

"You're so lucky I love you. I'll go because you are going and I won't be stuck dealing with my mom and her friends alone."

"Thanks, Patty! My agent wants me there because they have people who are a part of it and the dresses we're wearing are part of a line that I'll be modeling. They're ours to keep but there will be pictures taken and such, so be prepared."

"Let me see the dresses," I say trying to be excited for yet another night of dinner and drinks with a bunch of rich people who pretend to care about what's going on in my life.

We go out to her car to bring in her things as well as the dresses she's brought for us. She wants me to try mine on so she can be sure it fits before next week. I know it will because Bella knows my body as well as I do. Still, I appease her and try it on anyway. The dresses are both floor length. Mine is cream color with glitter all the way through. It is a halter top that is very low cut in the back so I won't be able to wear a bra. The slit in the front comes up to just above my knee. Bella is wearing a similar dress but hers is pale pink instead of cream. I slip the dress on and it is absolutely gorgeous. I hold the bottom up so it doesn't drag, and she pulls some shoes out of her bag. I'm in trouble because she brought me four-inch Louboutin heels to wear with it. My feet do not like four inch heels. However, the shoes match the material perfectly and the heel has some stones going up them that form a really pretty pattern.

Bella comes out in her dress and she looks beautiful. "Patty you look gorgeous in that dress," she gushes.

"Thanks, Bella, I feel pretty in this dress."

"I said gorgeous not pretty."

"You look pretty gorgeous yourself."

"Let's take a selfie and send it to your mom. She'll be so excited."

We take a selfie in our dresses then take them off so we don't ruin them.

"Now that I know your dress fits I'll take them back with me and I'll book us a spa day for that morning so we will be all set for the formal event that night."

"That sounds so great. Thanks, Bella."

"We'll have the works, mani/pedi, facials, hair and make-up. Your mom has a limo picking us up at my place at five."

I just nod, knowing she'll have all the details worked out. She'll call me with a time to be at her place and all I have to do is show up.

My phone buzzes a minute later.

Mom: You girls look beautiful.

Patty: Thanks Mom, see you at the fundraiser next week.

Mom: Thanks for coming.

Patty: ;-)

"You know you just made your mom's night right? Well, and mine," she says with a grin. "Now I don't have to endure this evening alone."

Once we're dressed in our comfy clothes we settle on the couch to play catch up.

"So tell me about this hottie next door," Bella says.

"I don't really know much about him. He's a handsome guy, well built, like he works out. He has a cute smile." My smile fades for a minute as I think back to the expression on his face that morning on the porch.

"What is it, Patty?"

"The other morning we were both sitting on our own porches doing our own thing and I noticed this expression come over his face. I feel like he was recalling a bad memory or something. Anyway, he's sporting a grunge look and he looked like he was in pain, but emotional pain not physical pain. I felt really bad for him."

"Do you know who he is?"

"I assume he's Mr. Montgomery's son because he looks a bit like him, though I don't know for sure."

"That might make sense. I think I remember him bragging about his son being in the Army."

I shrug. "Maybe. I feel like it's weird that I have never met him. We spent so much time up here when we were younger and I know Mr. and Mrs. Montgomery but have never met their son. And if I did, it was when I was young because I don't remember it."

"Actually, if you think about it, there weren't too

many times that they were here when we were."

"True." I make a mental note to ask my dad about it later.

Celia tells us that lunch is ready. Once we're seated at the table, we can see him from the window. He's sitting on his dock fishing. Suddenly he turns around, like he can sense us watching him.

"That's him, Mr. Montgomery's son," Bella says.

"How do you know?"

"We were at an event last year. You couldn't attend because of a book event. Your mom was in a bad mood and a bit bitchy to him. She said something about guys in the Army being too poor to make a good husband or something stupid like that."

"My mother really annoys me. The guy is defending her freedom to speak the shitty words that come out of her mouth and she bashes him."

She nudges me. "He was pretty hot in uniform."

I smile shyly. "He's pretty hot out of uniform." I blush because that hadn't come out the way I meant it.

We spend the remainder of the afternoon and evening watching chick flicks and doing girly things. Bella brought over some beauty products for us to do our own facials. We watched TV with goo all over our faces, laughing at a romantic comedy while we looked up pictures of pretty formal hairstyles for the fundraiser next week. We both saved a couple of styles we liked to show the salon when we get there.

We ate junk food and drank soda until after dinner then it was time to switch to wine. Celia was great to us. She cut us a great cheese and cracker tray with some grapes to have with our wine. She kept us fed and had tons of great munchies for us to enjoy during our girl's night. Bella was great about making sure I didn't think about my book or my agent once during the night. Sometime around midnight we got tired and passed out on opposite ends of the couch.

Carter

As I'm finishing my workout I notice a car pulling up to the house next door. I'm on immediate alert. Who the hell is this and is Patricia expecting someone? I try to see who is driving but the angle is off and I can't get a good view from this window. I sit perfectly still waiting for the person or people to move. A tall female gets out of the car and I swear I know her from somewhere. Since she's a female, I'm a bit less nervous but I still can't let my guard down. She walks right in without peeking in windows or making any signs of being a threat. I let it go as someone coming to visit. I'll keep an eye out though. I get a bottle of water and watch the house for any signs that something is wrong and once I see the princess and her friend come out together laughing, I know all is good. I wish I could just tell this woman that I'm here to protect her and to let me know if she's planning on having visitors so I don't have a heart attack when a fucking car pulls up. I take a shower and then throw some clothes into the wash because my room is starting smell foul from all of my gym clothes. I feel damn good now that I've hit the gym every day this week.

I decide I'll grab a bite to eat before going to the shed to gather my fishing gear. My dad and I have some great memories fishing out here. I wonder why I don't ever remember seeing Patricia here growing up. As a matter of fact, I feel like I never saw their family here. Why would my father and his friend both buy lake houses near each other but not spend time in them together? That just doesn't make any sense.

I shrug at my thoughts as I place my coffee and a bagel on the table and take a seat. I'm hoping by the time I'm done eating, my laundry will be done and then I can spend a little quiet time fishing.

When I finally get out to the dock, I have a thermos of coffee in hand, a bag of nuts for a snack, and all of my fishing gear. I'm happy to be able to just sit and enjoy the quiet. As I cast my first line, I think about the time my dad and I had gone out in his small boat. We weren't too far out but we had been fishing for a few hours. It was getting toward the end of the season and the water was cold. I discovered just how cold the water was when I tried to reel in a huge fish but lost my balance, falling into the water.

Smiling at the memory I get this sense like I'm being watched. I turn around to see if someone is there, but I see nothing. I chuckle and flash back to a time when I was overseas and one of my men thought I was crazy because I felt like we were being watched. I wasn't crazy, I was right. The same is true today. I turn again and when I do I have to squint to see them but Patricia and her friend are in the window watching me. I shake my head.

Yup, I still got it.

I reel in my line and cast it again. I start to think about how excited I am for this job opportunity and what I'll do if I don't get it. I really hope I do but if not, I need to find some other similar jobs to apply for. I feel a tug on my line so I reel in what I think is a fish, but when the hook comes out of the water I have caught nothing. I cast the line, remembering a particular weekend that my dad brought me out here, just the two of us. He was so awkward that weekend and when I finally got him to talk to me about what was going on he started stumbling through telling me about manhood. He laughed at me because I kept telling him I caught something and every time I would reel in my line it was empty. That was the weekend I told him I wanted to serve my country.

I was fourteen years old and had already made the decision. I was a freshman in high school and a recruiter had been at the school talking to students. I thought it was so cool that this guy was defending his country. He had been overseas twice. I spent an entire lunch period talking to him. That's when I decided I wanted to be like him.

Chapter 6

Patty

It's Saturday morning and I'm exhausted. I got back to my place late last night after being gone for two weeks. I did some cleaning up, fed my fish, and jumped in the shower before I crashed for the night. While I was lying in bed I couldn't help but think about how empty it is. My head has been filled with thoughts of the mystery man from the lake house. He has been invading my dreams from the moment he got to the lake house and last night I didn't sleep because I was thinking about him. I even had a date with B.O.B. because I needed to relieve some pressure.

I stretch in bed, trying to shake my thoughts of him because I'll probably never see him again. Even if I do go back to the lake house to finish writing what are the chances he will be there?

Joan is happy with what I've submitted and told me she can give me until the end of next month to get her another two or three chapters. Now I have to decide what I will do next, but first I need to get through this weekend and tonight's event.

I slide out of bed, slipping my feet into the slippers I keep by my nightstand, and go to the kitchen to make some coffee. I turn on my one cup coffeemaker and take a frozen breakfast sandwich from the freezer to heat up. I know how to cook and I don't mind it but it sucks to cook for one person. I often eat freezer meals just because it's easier. The microwave beeps and my coffeemaker finishes brewing me a perfect cup of coffee. I take both my coffee and breakfast sandwich to the living room to watch the news.

I don't watch TV often because I hate reality TV and there are always negative things on the news. I do watch for the weather and I want to see what the ten day forecast is going to be like before I think about going back to the lake house.

My cell buzzes; it's Bella.

Bella: Are you ready for some fun tonight?

Patty: We're going to have fun?

Bella: Aren't you funny. You know what I mean.

Patty: Hehehe, about as ready as I'll ever be. See you soon.

Bella: See you soon.

These events are more her and my mom's cup of

tea, but whatever, I'll go to please both of them. Hopefully I can have a good time and do some networking over my next book, which I have yet to name. As much as I hate to deal with snobby people at these events, I'm almost hoping to be recognized and have someone ask me about my last two books. I would love for my mom to see that I can be me and still be successful.

The weather forecast comes on just as I'm finishing my sandwich and I see the weather is getting cooler, but not so bad that I can't enjoy some more time at the lake. I try not to be there as it gets closer to winter because it can snow a lot and I don't want to get stuck. I put my dishes in the sink and go to take a shower. It only takes me a few minutes because I washed my hair last night and don't want to wash it again or it won't cooperate for the hairdresser later today. After I'm washed, I pack some clothes to sleep in tonight, as well as an outfit for tomorrow since I'm spending the night at Bella's.

I arrive at Bella's and she starts squealing like we're in high school again.

I roll my eyes. "Why do you get so excited over these events?"

"Because we get to get all dressed up, have our pictures taken, maybe do a little flirting, and of course do some networking for a new contract."

"Oh of course, don't forget the contract," I say sarcastically and she giggles, pulling me into her apartment.

Her place is so cute. It's a very open layout with a nice sized living room. On the other side of her living room is her kitchen. She has a huge snack bar that seats six and divides the kitchen from the living room. She has two bedrooms, which is really nice for nights like this. Her room is large, and has a huge walk in closet. She needs it because this woman has a serious wardrobe. She probably has more pairs of jeans than I do pants and skirts in my closet. I head into the spare room to put my bag away.

"I want to show you a new hairstyle I found for you," Bella says, then goes to get her laptop. I kind of liked the one we picked the other night but she wants me to see this one too.

She brings it up on the screen. "Check this out, Patty, it is perfect."

It *is* really pretty. My hair would be swept to the right and flow over my shoulder in curls.

"I like that. You can have a stylist do that to my hair."

"I'm so glad, because I already saved it to my phone hoping you would like it. I also got you this really pretty hair clip."

Even if I didn't like it she would convince me to do it anyway. She knows fashion better than I do and although she can be overpowering when it comes to me and the things I wear, I know she means well.

"What are you doing to your hair?" She brings up the picture for the style she chose and I have to say I'm a bit shocked because she is doing it similar to mine. Her hair is thicker than mine and the back of hers will be different but still the same idea.

"That is going to look really pretty on you, I

can't wait to see it."

"Thanks, are you ready to go? Our appointment is in thirty minutes and we are starting out with massages before we have lunch."

"Sure, let's roll." I wink at my friend, linking arms with her as we sashay out the door.

"I'll drive." She pulls her keys from her purse and we're off to the salon.

When we get there my mother is waiting in the lobby of the salon and I give Bella a look that screams *'What the fuck!'* She gives me a sympathetic look and I have a feeling my mother invited herself.

"Patricia, darling, how are you?"

"I'm fine, Mother."

"I'm so excited to have a girls' day with you two. I've booked us for a massage and after that they are going to serve us lunch. I've ordered us all a grilled chicken salad with dressing on the side, pita bread, and water with lemon." She looks so proud and I want to scream, I don't want a salad but I don't want to sound ungrateful so I just thank her for setting it up.

Three girls come out to the lobby and call our names. We follow them to our rooms and I'm happy to have the next forty-five minutes to myself. The woman tells me that she's going to give me a few minutes to get ready and she will be back, so I get comfortable on the table lying on my belly with my face through the pillow. I'm not sure why but my mind instantly goes to my mystery man. I haven't said anything to Bella and I can't help but wonder if he will be there tonight. She did say she saw him at an event of my mom's so maybe I will get to see him. I can only imagine how hot he will look in a tux, or even better, his dress uniform.

The masseuse knocks on the door to let me know she's coming in to get started. She tells me to let her know if she's applying too much pressure and she gets started rubbing the knots out of my back.

Forty-five minutes later she tells me I'm all set and that she'll meet me outside the door to take me back out to the lobby to meet up with my mom and Bella for lunch. It takes me all of two minutes to get dressed. She escorts me to the café where my mom and Bella are already there waiting for me with our salads in place.

"How was your massage, darling?"

"It was very relaxing. Thank you, Mother."

"My massage therapist was just okay. I've had better." Bella takes a bite of her salad.

"Oh don't be snobby, Bella." I give her a look because sometimes when she gets with my mom she starts to sound and act like her and that isn't how she really is. She grins because she knows I'm right. I often wonder if she does it to stay in my mother's good graces. I could care less about my mother and her graces.

We're eating in a comfortable silence until Bella says, "Sandra, is Mr. Montgomery's family attending tonight's event?" Bella asks my mother.

"I believe they are. Why do you ask?"

I'm giving Bella a look, because I'm going to fucking kill her if she says any more.

"Oh, I was just curious," she says with a huge grin on her face as she looks at me. She's lucky the waitress comes over to clear our empty plates and take us off to our pedicures because I'm about to pull her aside and tell her to cut the shit.

When we arrive at the section of the spa reserved for pedicures, my mother informs me that my ex will also be there tonight and he's looking forward to seeing me.

"Mother, we're done, I'm not looking forward to seeing him at all." I sit in my chair and stick my feet in the warm water.

"Oh, Patricia, he apologized, what more do you need from him?" she says, like him putting his hands on me is actually forgivable.

"Mother, how can you defend a man who hit your daughter? Do you remember the bruise I came home with? Not to mention I wasn't happy before he hit me. That was simply the last straw."

"I do, Patricia. He called me to explain what happened and said he apologized to you. He cares for you and he can take care of you. His family is very well off."

"That is really great for the next sucker he decides to put his hands on but it won't be me." I sigh and close my eyes, trying to relax and enjoy the rest of my spa day.

"Patricia, I—"

I put my hands up to silence her. "Mother, this conversation is over. I will never go back to him, now please let me enjoy the remainder of my spa day."

She sighs, but finally goes silent as the women get to work.

***

We're finally done at the spa and in the car on our way back to Bella's house to hang out until it's time to put on our dresses.

"I'm sorry, Patty. I should've warned you your mother was going to be there," she says once we are in her car. "She wanted to surprise you and I was afraid if I told you she was going to be there you would try to back out."

"I get that, but you still should have told me. I may have complained at first but I still would have gone. There's no way you would have let me back out of tonight anyway."

"You're right, I'm sorry, Patty. Do you still love me?" she whines and I can't help but laugh at her pout.

"I'll love you if you grab me a burger and fries on our way to your house. That salad sucked and I'm starving."

"You got it." She drives straight to the local fast food restaurant and orders my favorite combo meal. I know she feels bad because she even paid for it.

We pull up to her house and I practically run inside to eat my food.

"I hate that you can eat stuff like that and I can't," she says.

I shrug and shove more fries in my mouth. "I know you like being a model but no one told you to make that your career. I'm an author so I can eat what I want when I want. I just happen to be lucky that it doesn't affect my weight."

"Bitch," she mumbles jokingly, wandering off to

get some water while I finish up.

Once I'm done eating she tells me it's time for us to get dressed. After I toss my trash I find my dress laid out on the spare bed. Stepping into my gorgeous, flowing dress I go into the bathroom to check my hair and make sure I didn't mess up my make up while I devoured my burger and fries. I'm happy to see I just need to apply lipstick before I get into the limo.

Chapter 7

Carter

My interview was only yesterday, but I was offered the position on the spot. I officially start on Monday, but Derek, my new boss, mentioned it would be nice to be able to introduce me around. As the assistant director of our local veteran affairs office, I will always be attending events similar to this because we'll be looking for support and donations. I hate sucking up to snobby people for money. Derek will be there, as well as some of the other directors and assistant directors, but he said it was up to me if I decided to attend. My father says that means I should go and that he's testing me to see what I'll do in this situation.

I was dumb enough to mention that my parents are going, so of course that made it even harder for me to say no. I know it's a good opportunity to get my feet wet, so I told him I'd be there.

I'm hoping the fact that Patty and her friend were carrying dresses the other day and her mother is helping with this event means Patty will be there too. I don't know if I'll have the courage to introduce myself since I hadn't at the lake house. I'll at least watch for her, I bet she's going to look stunning.

There were several times when I really wanted to walk right up to her and just say, *'Hey, I'm Carter,'* but I was supposed to be there to watch her and I didn't want to have to lie to her about why I was there. I figured unless she approached me it would be best for me to stay away. If I do get to meet her I pray my father is right and she's more like Troy than Sandra.

I need to shave and clean up to put on my tux. Now that I'm retired my dress uniform stays neatly hung in my closet. My mom went out of her way to make sure I had a new tux that would fit me perfectly for this evening's event. I walk out of the bathroom now clean shaven, and of course I got a fresh haircut earlier today as well. If I'm going to be meeting co-workers, I want to look my best even if I don't feel my best.

"Carter, come have something to eat and then you need to get dressed," my mom calls up to me. When I'm halfway down the stairs she adds, "I made you something to eat so you won't be hungry since we won't be eating until much later this evening."

I smile at my mom, whom I adore by the way. "Thanks, Mom."

I sit to eat my huge sandwich and pile of chips. I may be really close to my dad from all the time we spent at the lake house, but my mom is one amazing woman. I can't imagine the fear my parents felt when they found out I was injured in Iraq. I know she's proud of me but I also know she is very happy that I'm no longer in the service so she doesn't have to worry anymore.

If only I could figure out how to get past the nightmares and move on with my life. Although they have lessened in frequency since I've started dreaming about my princess. I still have the nightmares once in a while.

I can't think about that right now, I need to finish my sandwich so I can get dressed because my mom's going to tell me any minute now that the limo driver will be here shortly.

"Carter, dear, how's your sandwich?"

"It's great, Mom."

"Good, finish up, sweetie. The limo driver will be here soon."

I chuckle to myself as I rinse my plate and place it in the dishwasher, then go to my room to finish getting ready.

***

The outside of the hotel is lined with photographers waiting to see who's going to make an appearance. With my father being owner of one of the most popular local banks, he is expected to show up to all of these events, and my mother and I are almost always by his side. We're waiting in the line of cars to pull up to the drop off spot. We finally get to the front and while we wait for the driver to open my dad's door he turns to me.

"Ready, son?"

"Yes, sir."

My mother smiles at me lovingly.

The door opens and we step out, but I wasn't prepared for my reaction to the flashes and the commotion from the reporters. It nearly sends me into a panic attack. I freeze as the flashes go off all around me and the reporters are screaming for us to turn in each of their directions so they can snap our picture. I'm on one side of my father and my mother is on the other, and they all want a picture of the Montgomery family. I start slipping, thinking the screams are my guys calling for help. Thankfully my father picks up that something is off and takes my arm.

"Son, are you okay?"

I shake my head. "Please get me inside."

He gives me a warm smile like he understands what I'm going through. "Plaster on a fake smile and I'll get you through this." I do my best to comply. Once we're inside he pulls me aside. "What happened?"

I take a few deep breaths. "The flashes and the loud commotion triggered a flashback. I think I'll be okay, thanks for getting me out of there, Dad."

"Anytime, son. Let's go get a drink." We head straight for the bar and he orders two scotches on the rocks.

I'm taking the first sip of my drink when my new boss Derek walks over.

"Looking good, Carter," he says, slapping me on the shoulder.

"Thanks, you should have seen me a minute ago.

I nearly lost it."

He too has PTSD and we spoke of our issues briefly during my interview. I have to admit it was great to talk to someone who has the same problem and not some lame doctor who pretends to understand what you're going through.

"Yeah the flashes from the cameras can get you good. That's one of those things you'll hopefully get over the more you're near them. Now that you know it affects you, you'll be able to prepare yourself next time."

"I haven't been to an event like this since I got home, so that was totally unexpected. Derek, I'm sorry I'm being rude. This is my father, Jackson Montgomery." I have no idea where my mom has taken off to but she does that to my dad often. She and the girls like to gossip.

Derek sticks his hand out. "Mr. Montgomery, it's a pleasure to meet you."

"Thank you for your service, Derek. The pleasure's all mine."

"If you don't mind, sir, I'd like to steal your son away for some introductions."

My father smiles proudly and nods as we walk away.

Derek introduces me to whirlwind of people, some of whom he tells me is a formality, and some he tells me to try to remember their names because I'm likely to bump into them again. One of them happens to be the head of veteran affairs for the entire state. Our office reports to him for anything we need or any issues we're having. Although I'm not easily intimidated, this guy does intimidate me slightly.

"Carter," Derek says, "this is, Tobey Hanson, the head of Veteran Affairs for the state."

"Ah, my new assistant director," he says as we shake hands.

"Yes, sir." I try not to look nervous, but it's hard because this dude is huge.

I mean, his tux looks like he could cross his arms and rip the damn thing and he has a deep, gravelly voice. The guy looks like he could chew me up and spit me out and I'm not a small guy.

"You'll be putting in a lot of hours while you learn your job and all of the benefits our veterans are entitled to," he says. "It's nice that you know some of the benefits already since you've been through some of it yourself, but there are a lot of things we offer soldiers that they don't know about." He sighs. "It kills me when I find out that our vets aren't getting the help they need, and being an MP you have the heart to help people. Being up there in rank you're used to dealing with soldiers of all ranks. Just know that in the near future I expect to be able to call you with an issue and you be able to tell me what you can do to help me out."

I smile up at him. "Sir, my training has made me a problem solver and helping our men and women is something I'm looking forward to. I wanted to continue to serve our country, but my body won't allow it, so this is probably the next best way I can help."

He nods. "Glad to hear it. You two enjoy the rest of your night."

When we walk away from him, I release a breath

I hadn't realized I was holding and Derek laughs.

"He's really a giant teddy bear, but he likes to play tough with all the newbies. Although you do have a lot to learn, he isn't a hard ass like he says he is. I'll tell you, though, he is extremely passionate about helping our vets, so he really will want you to learn all the benefits we can give our men and he'll expect you to go out of your way to make sure they get them."

I take another deep breath. "Good to know."

Patricia

When the limo pulls up outside of Bella's apartment I have to admit I'm slightly excited. I haven't been out for some fun in a long time. Although this isn't my ideal night out, I'm still hoping to enjoy myself. We walk down the stairs to our waiting car and the driver has the door open for us.

"Good evening, ladies. Ms. Fitzgerald-Carmichael will meet you at the fundraiser. She's already there waiting," he tells us.

I nod in acknowledgement and we slide into the back of the huge car. There really was no need for a limo, a regular car would have been fine but my mom loves to go above and beyond.

As we pull away, Bella breaks out a bottle of champagne and pours us each a glass. I'm so grateful because I could use some liquid courage. I'm a bit nervous about seeing Ben and secretly hoping to see my mystery man.

"To a fun girl's night," she says, clinking her

glass with mine.

"Hear, hear," I say, downing half the glass. She giggles and pours me more.

When we pull up to the hotel there's a long line of cars waiting to let people out so we finish off another glass of champagne and place our glasses back in the holders. Our driver arrives at the red carpet drop off spot and calls back to us, "Ready, ladies?"

"About as ready as I'll ever be," I say.

He climbs out of the front seat and walks around to open my door. When I climb out I'm flooded with flashes and questions. I plaster a wide smile on my face and wait for Bella to get out of the car behind me. We hook arms and step into our signature pose for the cameras. Bella eats this up. She's blowing them kisses and striking poses with me, while they're trying to get my attention.

"Ms. Fitzgerald, is it true you've started your next book?" someone calls from the crowd.

"Maybe, where did you hear that?"

"It's all over social media." He says it like I should know and I do, however, it's fun to mess with them.

I chuckle. "I have, but I'm not prepared to give a timeframe. I won't give my readers information I do not have. Since you follow me on social media you can get the updates there." I wink at the photographer and we walk to the other side of the red carpet to pose for some more photos.

"Ms. Fitzgerald, can you give us an idea as to what your next bestseller's about?"

I glance at Bella with a look of shock, and

respond, "My next book is a bestseller and I haven't even written it yet." She bursts out laughing and I turn back to him. "I'm sorry, I'm not releasing that information yet. As I told your friend over there, stay tuned for more info."

We walk the remainder of the way up the red carpet smiling and waving the whole way. Once inside I whisper, "Thank fuck that is over. I'm going to kick my agent's ass for telling them I was going to be here. It's way too early for this type of questioning."

Bella shakes her head. "Let's get a glass of wine."

We're making our way to the bar for a glass of wine when my mother approaches. "Patricia, darling, I'm so glad you girls were able to make it," she gushes.

"Like I had a choice," I mumble under my breath. "Hello, Mother," I say louder. "Has Father arrived?"

She sighs heavily. "How would I know? I don't track your father, but I can tell you that Ben is here and is looking forward to seeing you."

"Mother, I wish you would stop tracking Ben as well. You really need to get over this. I have no desire to see him and you need to quit forcing him on me. It isn't going to happen."

I cringe when I see him approaching, and someone else calls my name. I turn to see Brooke coming over, surely to discuss my next book. She is a big time blogger and promotion expert. She works with only bestsellers to make sure their books are heavily promoted. While I am greeting her Bella excuses herself to go network and find her next big contract.

Brooke air kisses both my cheeks.

"Mother, excuse us, please," I say and walk away, unhappy with her attempt to hook me back up with that asshole.

"Joan tells me you have submitted a few chapters of your next book," Brooke says, practically drooling over getting the promo deal.

"I have but it's really nowhere near done. She's rushing me and doesn't realize that only makes it harder to write."

"You know how it is in this business. The readers want fresh stuff to read and we need great authors like you to provide it!"

"Thank you, and I'm glad you're enjoying my writing, but like I told Joan it takes time and she has to let me do my thing. I'll definitely have her touch base with you about a promo deal when the time comes, though."

"I would really appreciate that. I know you weren't too happy with the last promo company your agent used and I would love the opportunity to work with you."

"Touch base with Joan this week. Tell her that you and I spoke tonight and that I promised you the chance to bid on the promo of the next book. Show her what you've got and what your ideas are and I'll set up a meeting with her to go over it."

"Thank you so much, Ms. Fitzgerald."

"I'm not promising we'll pick you, but we'll at least discuss it. Now if you'll excuse me, I see my father and I would like to go say hi."

"Of course, have a great night!"

I'm halfway across the room to speak to my father when Ben steps in front of me. "Patricia, why are you ignoring me?"

"That's simple, I have nothing to say to you, Ben."

"You may have nothing to say to me, but I have a lot to say to you. I really wish you would hear me out. You know you still want me. I know you haven't been with anyone since we broke up. I bet you're hoping I'll come crawling back to you, begging for forgiveness," he says, stepping closer to me.

My brows shoot up in shock. "You disgust me. You think because you're attractive and you have your daddy's money you can put your hands on a woman and then just apologize and all will be okay. Well let me tell you, I don't care how attractive you are or how much money you have. No one puts their hands on me. We're through."

I quickly make my escape, walking up to my father. "Daddy!" I call out to get his attention.

He hugs me. "How are you, pumpkin?"

"I'm good, Daddy.

"You look stunning," he says proudly.

"Thanks, Daddy. You're looking quite handsome yourself."

"Thanks, pumpkin. What is going on with you and Ben?" he asks full of concern.

I roll my eyes. "He can't understand that we're done. I don't want to see him anymore and he seems to think he can convince me otherwise."

He shakes his head and I change the subject.

"Daddy, is your lake house being used at all over the next few months?"

"No, pumpkin, it's all yours. I just want to know when you will be there so I can check on you."

"You mean like the man you put in Mr. Montgomery's house?" I raise my eyebrow at him.

"I don't know what you're talking about."

"Oh you don't, huh?"

He's saved by the announcement that it's time to take our seats for dinner. He wraps his arm through mine and escorts me over to our table where Bella is already seated. We take our seats and get started on our salad course. While we eat, there are guest speakers up on stage talking about the woman's shelter my mother is helping to raise money for. I think this is what pisses me off the most about my mother. She supports such an amazing cause like a woman's shelter then tells me I should forgive Ben for hitting me. Could she be any more of a hypocrite? I mean, really.

Bella leans in to my side. "A penny for your thoughts."

"I was just thinking about how hypocritical it is that my mother supports such a great cause but wants me to forgive Ben for hitting me. I just don't get it."

"She's not like you, Patty. Your mom needs money and stability, so she needs rich men in her life to take care of her."

"That's fine for her but I'm happy making my own money. Listen, let's just drop it. I don't want to ruin the night and I still haven't told my father what really happened. This is not the place for him to find out." She agrees and we continue enjoying our meal.

One of my father's friends from across the table says, "Patty, did I hear you telling the media you've started on your next book?"

"I didn't have much choice since I posted it on my Facebook page and my agent is quick to tell the world. They were fishing for release dates and I'm only in the beginning stages of writing the book. It will be a bit still, but yes I have started on it."

"Good for you. I hear your last two books are doing quite well."

"Yes they are, thank you," I say with pride.

I shove food in my mouth as he starts questioning Bella on her work and what she has coming up. She tells him that she has a swimsuit ad and then she'll be working a jean ad for the fall.

A short while later dinner is done and a band starts to play. My dad turns to me and asks for a dance and of course I agree. He has a concerned look on his face.

"What's wrong, Daddy?" I ask.

"I'm just trying to figure out why you weren't so excited to talk about the book you're working on. Usually you're beaming about it and elated to discuss your story. I haven't once heard you talk about the plot or the characters or anything."

"I don't know, something feels off with this one. I don't know if it's because Joan is rushing me or what, but I have to figure it out and make a decision on what to do with it."

"If you're not happy with your agent, then get rid of her ass and get someone else. This is your work and you need to love it so your passion will flow."

"Thanks, Daddy, I'll think about it. I promise."

Just as I finish telling him that, there is a tap on his shoulder and it's Ben asking if he can cut in. Ben clearly knows I didn't tell my father what happened, because my father would have killed him. My father graciously steps aside as Ben takes my hand and pulls me close to him.

"What do you want, Ben?"

We start to dance. We move well together on the dance floor. We didn't move so well together in bed.

"To have a few moments alone with you to talk," he says as we sway to the music. He starts leading me further and further from my father and before I know it we are near the edge of the dance floor.

"You do realize there is nothing to discuss," I say. Apparently he disagrees because he grabs my elbow and yanks me out of the room. "Ben, stop. You're hurting my arm."

He sneers at me. "Will you stop being a brat and just come talk to me?" I can smell the alcohol on his disgusting breath.

"Maybe when you're sober," I say, snatching my arm from his grip. He grabs it again and tries to pull me to a corner where no one can see us. Most of the party is in the other room, so there are no witnesses.

"I said we're going to talk and I meant it. Now let's go." He tries to grab my arm one more time, almost causing me to trip in my ridiculously high shoes, but before he can, a man appears and stops him.

"I believe the lady said she's all set."

"Who the fuck are you?" Ben snaps and I can see that the man is pissed because he's clenching his teeth, the muscles in his jaw tightening.

"The person who's going to teach you some manners. Now step away from the lady."

Oh my, it's the guy from the lake. It dawns on me that I know his face. Granted, it's clean shaven and his hair is shorter, but I recognize his eyes. They're a bright hazel that anyone one who's ever really looked at them would never forget.

Ben approaches him with his fists clenched like he really wants to fight him here in public, "I don't know who you think you are, but this is between me and my girl," he says.

Before he can do anything, Ben's father appears. "Ben, cut the shit."

"Father, this guy is trying to take my girl from me."

"I'm not your girl and I haven't been since you decided it was okay to slap me." I gasp and cover my mouth. Oh shit, I can't believe I just said that out loud. I run toward the door and my mystery man comes running after me.

"Wait," he says, "Are you all right?"

I take a deep breath to try and compose myself, but I'm not sure it's working because I'm shaking like a leaf. "Who are you?" I say, turning to face him. "My father sent you to the lake didn't he? Did he send you to watch over me tonight too?"

He sighs and looks slightly embarrassed. "The lake house yes, tonight no. I saw that creep pulling on you and I didn't like the way he was treating you."

"That creep is my ex who enjoys a few too many drinks at these events. I'll be fine, thanks." I'm being incredibly rude, but I'm embarrassed that he witnessed the scene and that I admitted to being slapped around by my ex. The only people who know are Bella and my mom.

"I guess I'll leave you be then," he says, and turns to leave.

"Wait, I'm sorry. I'm being a total bitch and I don't mean to." I pause as I try to gain some control. My voice softens, "I'm Patricia. My friends call me Patty."

He turns back with a gorgeous glowing smile that lights up his face. "Carter," he says. "It's nice to finally meet you, Patty. I wanted to introduce myself at the lake house, but I didn't want to intrude."

"Thanks, I appreciate that."

"What's up with this ex of yours? Did he really hit you?"

"Unfortunately yes. We were at an event like this one night and he had gotten a bit drunk and when I asked him to slow down with the drinking he dragged me out of the room and backhanded me." I look down, no longer able to look into his eyes. "He told me that no woman was going to dictate to him what he could and couldn't do. He told me to take my place at his side and be his arm candy the way I'm supposed to. I told him to fuck off and I left. I sent him a text telling him we were done and that I never wanted to see him again."

"Good for you. That's awesome." He's staring at me proudly.

"What's your story? You're Mr. Montgomery's son, right?"

"You got it. I'm here representing the Veteran's Affairs office. I work for them starting Monday."

"That's pretty awesome too. What are you doing for them?"

"I'm the new assistant director for the local office. There are several throughout the state and we come to these events to make our presence known so when we need help we can get it."

"That sounds like a pretty great job. You must be excited."'

"I am." He pauses like he's mulling something over. "Hey, what do you say we blow this joint and go get a coffee?"

I raise my eyebrows. "In an evening gown and tux?"

"I don't care if you don't."

"Let me get my purse." He walks me back into the room where I left my purse sitting on our table. Bella is sitting there talking with some people I don't know.

"Excuse me one moment," I say, interrupting their conversation. "Bella, I'm taking off, but I will text you later."

She sees Carter behind me and whispers, "You better."

I grin. "Carter, let's go before my mother tries to stop me."

While we're walking out he says, "I had my father follow me here earlier to drop off my Jeep. We can take that if it's alright with you."

"That's fine. We took a limo here so my car is at

Bella's house because I was supposed to be spending the night at her house, but I think I'll just go home after."

"I'll drop you off at your car when we're done."

"Thanks."

He takes my hand to help me climb into the passenger's seat of his Jeep. His touch sends goosebumps spreading throughout my body. He gets in on his side and drives off. "Where does Bella live?" he asks.

When I tell him her address we decide to go to a quiet cafe up the street from her house. Claire's is great because they have good coffee and they do things like poetry night and standup comedy nights for people who are just starting out and want to practice. I've gone there before to write for a change of scenery. I find admiring the people sometimes inspires me.

We pull up to Claire's and there are people here but it wasn't overly packed for a Saturday night. He gets out and walks around to my side, opening my door for me and taking my hand to help me climb out so I won't fall in my dress. I feel an electric shock flow between us that makes me smile, however, I ignore it, not sure what it is or if he feels it too.

We walk into the cafe and all eyes are on us because we are dressed in formal attire. We order our coffee and then secure a seat in a far corner.

"So what's really up with the loser at the fundraiser?" he asks.

"Like I said before, he's my ex. He doesn't want to accept that we're done."

"That sucks. Hopefully his loss is my gain." He shows me his gorgeous smile.

I blush, thinking to myself *what a flirt*. I want to change the subject so I say, "What's up with you?"

"Like I told you at the event, I start working for the Veterans Affairs office on Monday, but I mainly go to the fundraisers to support my parents. As I'm sure you know they own Central Bank, and they go to these events to keep up appearances and get customers for the bank."

"That's sweet."

"I owe it to them. They have done a lot to support me since I've been home and had to deal with my knee injury. It's the least I can do."

I recall the pained look on his face at the lake house. "I'm sorry you had to deal with that entire situation."

"It's okay, to be honest. I'm sorry I got hurt because I loved my job and miss it. I had my own section of men and we worked well together. We went on some crazy missions but we saved quite a few lives. If it weren't for my knee I would still be over there and not here having a conversation with you dressed in a tux." He shrugs. "I guess that makes one good thing to come out of my injury."

"Are you trying to make me blush?" I ask, taking another sip of my coffee.

He laughs. "I wasn't, but it was cute when you did it the first time, so why not?"

I slap his hand playfully and the jolt I felt when he helped me out of the car returns.

I yawn, and he says, "Looks like you need to get home before I put you to sleep."

"I'm sorry, Carter. My mother tires me out with all the prepping she makes me do before these events. Besides, it's getting late and we've been sitting here for a while."

"No problem. Come on, gorgeous, I'll take you home as long as you promise I can call you."

I giggle as and slip my phone out of my purse. "Text yourself from my phone, that way we'll have each other's numbers."

He does it and then hands it back to me. He takes my hand and we walk back to his Jeep so he can take me to Bella's. As he pulls away I give him directions to her house. I pull out the keys to my car, thankful I didn't leave my keys inside her place or I'd have to go back to the event.

When he pulls up to her house he gets out and runs around to my side of the Jeep, opening the door for me yet again and helping me out. He walks me to my car and when we reach it he says, "Thanks for having coffee with me."

I smile. "Thanks for buying me coffee."

"So, can I see you again sometime soon?" he asks, sounding very unsure of himself.

"I think I'd like that." I look down to hide the blush that's creeping up.

"Great, I'd like to take you to dinner Monday night after I get out of work."

"Sure," I say, looking up at him with a shy smile.

He's looking into my eyes, like he wants to make a move, but is unsure of himself. He leans in and kisses me on the cheek. "In you go. I want to make sure you get in safely."

I unlock the door and climb inside, giving him a

brief wave before he pulls away.

Chapter 8

Patty

What the hell is that buzzing noise?

I stretch in my bed looking around trying to figure out what the hell is going on. Then I realize someone's at my door. I look at the clock. 10:30 a.m. Holy shit, I slept late. I jump out of bed as the buzzer rings yet again. I run to the speaker and press the button.

"Who is it?" I shout angrily.

"Me, let me in!" Bella screams into the speaker. I press the button to let her up. She's going to kick my ass because I just realized I never texted her last night. A minute later I flinch when she starts pounding on my front door.

"Hold your horses!" I shout as I open it.

"I'll text you, you said. I'll call you, you said. Did I get either? *No!* Do you realize I was worried about you all night?" she screams, pacing my living room.

"I was with Carter, not Ben. I don't know why

you were so worried. I said I would call you so I could tell you how it went. Sorry I didn't realize you would be so worried."

"How come you two left last night?"

"Oh my God! I didn't even get to tell you what happened." I sit on the couch.

"So you going to fill me in or leave me in suspense?"

"While you were networking, Ben stepped in on my dance with my father and led me off the dance floor without anyone noticing. When we were close enough to the door, he grabbed my arm and pulled me out of the room to try and talk."

"Are you serious?"

I nod. "He started to hurt me, so I pulled my arm away and told him there was nothing to talk about. He disagreed and pulled me completely out of the room. We continued our arguing and while we were going back and forth, Carter saw what was happening and came to my rescue."

Now she's glowing. "Are you serious?"

I give her a look. "Are you going to say anything more than, 'Are you serious?'"

She laughs. "Sorry. What happened next?"

"The two of them had words from a distance and when Ben was approaching Carter for a fight, Ben's father came out and stopped him. The worst part was I slipped about him backhanding me to his father."

She gasps. "No way! What did his father say?"

I shrug. "I didn't stick around to find out. Carter followed me and introduced himself. I was a bitch for about a minute, then we started talking and it was like we clicked. He wants to see me again. He asked me when he dropped me off last night if we could do dinner and we exchanged numbers."

"I've never seen you like this. You're absolutely glowing," she says, and that's when I realize my cheeks hurt from smiling. "So what did you tell him?"

"I asked him if he was picking me up or if we were meeting somewhere."

"And? Don't leave me hanging."

I burst out laughing. "He's picking me up tomorrow night at six thirty." I'm giddy with excitement. "We have to go pick you out an outfit to wear!"

We run to my room and start going through all the clothes in my closet. Then I realize, "Hey, how do I know what to wear when I don't know where he's taking me?"

"Text him and ask him."

When I turn on my phone, I notice I already have a text from him.

Carter: Good morning! Hope you slept well.

Patty: I slept a little too well, just woke up about fifteen minutes ago. How about you?

Carter: I got up around eight to work out.

Patty: You work out on Sundays?

Carter: It depends on my mood and I was trying to occupy my mind because I kept thinking

about someone.

Oh my God. "Look what he just wrote."
I show Bella the text and she squeals. "That's awesome," she says, excited for me.

Patty: *blushing*

Carter: I bet, you're cute when you're blushing.

Patty: Are you trying to make it worse on purpose? Where are we going for dinner tomorrow? I need to know how to dress.

Carter: Lol, No I'm not and dress comfortable. Like you did at the lake house ;-)

Patty: Ugh! I got to go. I'll talk to you later.

Cater: Yes you will. Have a good day!

Patty: You too!

When I look up from my phone Bella is leaning against my bureau with her arms crossed, tapping her foot, like I've done something wrong.
"What?"
"Girl you're redder than a beet, what was all of that?" I laugh and give her my phone so she can read the conversation. Between the two of us, we decide on a pair of jeggings with a cute sweater and a pair of Uggs.
Once we're done picking my clothes, Bella says,

"Go take a shower and let's go to lunch."

***

It's Monday morning and I'm lying in bed exhausted because I barely slept a wink last night. All I kept thinking about was my date with Carter tonight. He looked so hot the other night in his tux. I kept dreaming about him stripping it off painstakingly slowly. I wanted him to rip it off and he wouldn't. When he was finally done he climbed over me like I was his prey and that's when I woke up soaked with my want for him.

Fuck this.

I reach over into my nightstand and grab my bullet. I turn it on and rub it gently over my clit thinking of Carter. I'm imagining his large hands rubbing all over my body and his full, luscious lips kissing my neck and collarbone. It's been so long since anyone has touched me that I'm coming in a matter of minutes. My legs shaking, I ride it out with my bullet pressed between my legs.

I groan in frustration. It's only helped a little, and I still have to manage to get some work done before we go out tonight.

I send him a text.

Patty: Good luck on your first day!

Carter: Thanks! Hope you have a good day too!

Patty: Thanks! I can't wait to see you tonight.

Carter: Me too ;-)

I jump out of bed and hit the shower so I can go about my day. When I'm done, I make a cup of coffee and boot up my laptop to see what's going on in the social media world. I Google my name to see if there are pictures posted from the event Saturday since my agent loves seeing me out in public. I find pictures of me with Bella getting out of the limo and posing on the red carpet. Captioned under a nice pic of me and Bella is,

Author P. A. Fitzgerald with model friend Bella Campbell at a fundraiser Saturday night.

I print that one out. I have a best friend's frame that I switch the picture out on once in a while and that's a nice one. I continue scrolling through the pictures when I come across a picture of me and Carter and I'm mesmerized. The caption reads,

Author P. A. Fitzgerald leaves event with mystery man, believed to be the son of Mr. Montgomery, local bank owner.

I'm all smiles because we're looking at each other and smiling like we've known each other for years and yet we only just met. My phone rings, startling me from my thoughts, I look at my phone and roll my eyes.

"Good morning, Mother."

"Patricia, darling, how could you take off on Ben like that Saturday night? There are pictures of you and that boy all over social media and people are talking."

"Mother, stop!" I snap. "I did not run out on Ben, he backhanded me and I broke up with him. Stop feeding him false hope that we will get back together because we will *not*. I don't care if he is the president of the United States, I'm not going back to him. And for your information I left with Carter because he came to my rescue when Ben got drunk and nearly attacked me yet again outside the event. Please stop defending this man."

"Patricia, I'm your mother, you need to calm down."

"That's right, you're my mother, so how about you start sticking up for *me* because the fundraiser we attended that night took place because of men like Ben? When you're ready to stop pushing him on me, call me. Until then I have nothing more to say, Mother!"

I hang up the phone panting with anger. I want to scream. My phone starts ringing again and it's her but I send her to voicemail, refusing to take her call. She calls again and this time I put her to voicemail and then send her a text.

Patty: *I'm working right now. I can't have this conversation with you.*

Mother: *I'm sorry.*

I ignore her text and move on to my email, and of course I have one from my agent. All it says is ***"Who's the stud?"*** I send her a brief reply telling her I will let her know if he becomes someone significant, though right now he's just a date. I answer a few other emails and then get to work on my writing.

A short while later I realize I haven't eaten anything yet. I take a break to eat and check my social media. I make myself a sandwich, chips, and some grapes then plop myself back in front of the laptop to see what's going on. When I open my fan page there are a ton of posts asking who my mystery man is and if it's serious. I sigh, realizing I need to give Carter a heads up about this. I send him a text so I don't bother him if he's super busy at work.

Patty: Hey can you call me when you have a free moment?

Carter: Only if you promise it's not to back out on me.

Patty: I promise

A minute later my phone rings. "Hey, Carter, how's your day going?"

"Good so far, and I'm hoping it will stay that way," he chuckles.

"Well, that depends. I logged on to check my social media and chat with my readers and I discovered something. I'm not sure how you will feel about it."

"You mean our picture all over the place and everyone asking who your mystery man is?"

"You know?" I question, slightly nervous.

He laughs. "Yeah one of my buddies saw it and called me this morning. Listen, I know we don't really know each other and we're only going on our first date, but I could care less. Let them post what they want."

"I'm glad you're not upset about being my 'hot mystery man' as one paper posted."

"Are *you* mad that I'm your hot mystery man?"

I blush because I know he's flirting with me. "No."

"You're blushing, aren't you?"

I shake my head, though he cannot see it. "I should let you get back to work."

"I'll take that as a yes and see you at six thirty."

"Talk to you later, Carter."

I cut the call and debate if I should post something about last night's photo. I decide to tell my fans that for now I'm keeping his identity a secret, but may decide to introduce him in the future.

With all that's going on around me I can't focus on the book so I take a break to simply read and relax for a while before I have to get ready for my date with Carter. As I sit on the couch with a book to read, my mind is wandering to ideas for my book. Now I can't even focus on reading. I hate days like this. I can't seem to focus on any one thing. I jot down my ideas in my notebook, toying with the scene on paper until I have it the way I want it. I make note of roughly where I want it to go in the book and once I'm satisfied I decide to start getting ready.

A short while later I'm pacing my living room ready for my date and nervous as heck. It's been a long time since I've been on a date.

He was so sweet the other night. I smile as I recall us leaving the dinner in his Jeep to go for coffee. He was a complete gentleman, opening doors and buying me coffee and a muffin. We chatted a bit about everyday life and kept the conversation light since it was late and we had both had a long day. The way he looked at me when I spoke was like he was truly interested in what I had to say and he wanted to hear more. I thought it was so sweet that he kissed me on the cheek before ushering me into my car so he could make sure I got off safely.

My thoughts are interrupted when the buzzer to my apartment rings. I'm so deep in thought it makes me jump. I get up and answer it. "Hello?"

"Hey, it's me," Carter says, and I buzz him in. Minutes later he's knocking on my door.

I open it to find him smiling at me with a small bouquet of flowers in his hand. "Hi, these are for you," he says, handing them to me.

"Thank you, they're really pretty. I'll just put them in some water and we can go."

"Cool. I thought we would go to Jake's. Have you ever been there?"

I turn to him with a smile that shows how happy I am about his choice. "Yes, I love Jake's. How'd you know?"

"I didn't. I just figured after getting dressed up this weekend it would be nice to have a casual, relaxing dinner."

"That's perfect because to be honest, I'm not a fan of getting too dressed up. I do it to please my mother." I put my flowers in water.

"I've had the...pleasure of meeting your mom on a few occasions."

"If I know my mom, I'm sure it was no pleasure." I laugh. "I'm ready if you are."

"Sure, I'll drive," he says, opening the door for me and we make our way down to the car hand in hand.

Being the gentleman that he is, Carter opens the door to his Jeep for me so I can climb in. I'm sitting there fidgeting, my leg jumping, when he gets into the driver's seat. I don't realize I'm doing it until he places his hand on my leg. "Relax," he says. His strong, warm hand feels good on my leg. His touch sends goosebumps all over my body. I look down, biting my lip as I'm blushing.

He puts his key in the ignition and starts the car. As he drives off I can't help but wonder what this incredible man sees in me. I glance over for a moment while he's focused on driving. His car is filled with his musky, minty scent and it's intoxicating.

He senses me staring so he looks over. "A penny for your thoughts."

I can't answer him right now. Turning my head, I look back out the window. "Trust me, you don't want in my head."

"Oh, but I do," he says.

A minute later we pull up to Jake's. He finds a spot immediately and gets out of the Jeep to open my door. I'm nervous and my clumsiness has me practically falling out of the Jeep and into his arms. My body instantly warms as he catches me and looks into my eyes. We stay like that for what feels like forever, but we are broken from our trance when a lunatic screeches into the parking lot.

"Let's go eat," he says. "I'm starved."

When we get inside he gives his name and we're instantly seated with two menus and water. I love Jake's because they offer breakfast all day and I love having breakfast for dinner. Carter picks up his menu, but when he notices I'm not really looking at mine he says, "Let me guess, you know what you want."

"I do. I love their breakfast and always have it when I come here, no matter what time of day it is. I'm having the special. It's two eggs, two pieces of bacon, home fries, and a pancake."

"That sounds good. I think I'll have the same thing."

"I can never finish it but I get a little of everything I love."

He closes his menu and leans on the table to start a conversation when our waitress comes over. "What can I get you two tonight?"

"I would like a coffee with the breakfast special," I say.

She grins at me. "Will you ever order anything else, Patty?"

I laugh. "Maybe someday. I'd like my eggs whites only and scrambled with—"

"Broccoli, peppers and onions. Got it."

I giggle as she turns to Carter for his order.

"I'll make it easy on you," he says, "make it

two."

She looks back to me with a sneaky smile and walks off with our order.

"What was that all about?" Carter asks me.

"What?" I feign innocence. "I saw the look she gave you."

I shrug. "I'm usually in here alone. It sucks to cook for one person and this place isn't far from me so I come here anytime I feel like having breakfast. I always order the same thing, the same way, every time."

"That's pretty funny," he says. Our waitress returns with our coffee. Once she's gone he asks, "Why are you and your mom not on the best terms?"

I sigh, not sure I want to talk about this. I give him the short answer. "She wants me to be someone I'm not. She thinks that just because Ben apologized and he has money I should forgive him and go back to him. He's boring and not very nice, so why I would do that is beyond me."

"No offense, but she's a bit..." he hesitates, trying to choose his words carefully.

"Snobby," I answer for him.

He chuckles. "Yeah, I guess that's a way to describe her."

"She's very snobby. I've never spoken to my father about why they separated but I think it was because she wanted someone with more money. My stepfather was one of the top lawyers around and is now the district attorney, plus he comes from money. My mother likes to be his arm candy and believes that as her daughter it is my place to follow in her footsteps, playing the supportive wife who does whatever her husband bids."

"I wanted to flatten your ex Saturday night. I can't believe your mother supports a great cause like a battered woman's shelter but wants you to be with a man who hits you and treats you that way."

"I know, I thought the same thing. Anyway, can we shift the conversation? I'd rather not talk about her anymore."

"Sure, I'm sorry. I didn't realize it was such a heavy topic," he says with an apologetic smile.

"How come I've never seen you at the lake house?"

He shrugs. "I was wondering the same thing, but I figured it was an age gap or just happened we weren't there at the same times."

"My mom hates the place so I really didn't start spending time there until I was about twelve or thirteen. My mom always hated that my dad took me there but I loved it so I didn't care."

"Yeah, and like I said, I think I'm a few years older than you so I was probably over hanging at the lake house with my dad at that point. Although I have to admit I did enjoy being back there."

"Why how old are you?" I ask, curious. He doesn't look that old.

He grins as our waitress delivers our food and when she walks away he says, "I'll tell you my age if you tell me yours."

I can't help the giggle that escapes me. "Okay, fair enough."

"I'm thirty but I'll be thirty-one soon."

"Yeah, you were probably over the lake house

then, because I'm only turning twenty-five, so you're about six years older than me."

"I was still going, but not nearly as much," he says.

We both start eating in a comfortable silence, enjoying our dinner. About halfway through he says, "This is really good, I'm glad I got it."

"I'm glad you like it. I would have felt bad if you picked my favorite meal and decided it sucked."

"Nah, you have good taste."

The waitress comes over to ask if we need anything else. I tell her that I'm good and he does the same, so she drops the bill and as I go to take it he grabs it and says, "I got this."

"But you paid Saturday night."

He raises his eyebrows like he can't believe I just said that. "And I'll pay next time too."

"How do you know there will be a next time?" I tease him.

"Because I'm about to ask you when can I see you again." He drops some money on the table. "Do you want to do something else or do you want to just go hang out?"

"How do you feel about a movie at my place?"

"I like it," he says, taking my hand and pulling me from the booth.

When we get back to my place I unlock the door and hit the light. "Have a seat and I'll get us some drinks. What would you like?"

"Water is fine," he says, sitting on the loveseat across from the TV.

I go to the kitchen for two bottles of water and then join him on the loveseat. I have Netflix and On

Demand so we can watch pretty much anything. He leans forward to put his water on a coaster on my coffee table and I can feel him staring at me. I glance over and notice he's inched closer. The back of his fingers brush a piece of hair from my face and he whispers, "I really like you, please tell me you'll see me again."

I'm mesmerized by his eyes so a nod is all I can accomplish before his full lips gently press to mine in a kiss. He hovers for a moment waiting for permission to continue. I press my lips to his. He sticks his tongue out, gently licking my lips. I open my mouth to him and our tongues gently caress one another's.

It's a soft, sweet kiss that has me instantly wet for him. I haven't been touched like this in so long and his warm, strong hands are rubbing up and down my leg.

He breaks our kiss. "You have no idea how long I've been waiting to do that." He presses his forehead to mine in an attempt to gain some control, but I want more.

"How about you do it again?" I suggest, looking into his eyes.

He gives me what I want, though this time his hand goes to the nape of my neck and he deepens the kiss. With a moan I climb over his lap and continue to kiss him. He runs his hands up my back and presses me against his lean, hard body. I love that he's in shape but not huge, because we fit perfectly together.

I break away, panting. "I'm sorry, I'm not sure what's come over me. I'm not usually like this." I look into his eyes. "There's just something about you that makes me feel comfortable and safe."

"It's okay, but we should slow down. I don't want you to have any regrets. I need to spend some time looking for an apartment this week, but I really want to see you. Why don't I take you out Friday night? We can do whatever you want." I bite my lip and nod. "That sounds great."

He picks me up off the couch with him as he stands, placing me on my feet. Slipping his hand over my cheek, he leans in to give me a chaste kiss. "I think I should go, but I'll talk to you soon." I can see the concern on his face as he fights to maintain control.

"Okay," I say with a smile, walking him to the door.

Chapter 9

Patty

It's Thursday morning and thanks to distractions I've barely done any writing this week. I've gone shopping and had lunch with Bella to fill her in on my date with Carter. He has been on my mind way more than writing and unfortunately, so has my mother. She's been texting me and calling me all week, basically begging for me to stop ignoring her. She wants me to call her so we can discuss Ben and what happened at the event on Saturday night.

I make a fresh cup of coffee and sit down at my laptop to go through my social media and see what my followers and friends are up to. I'm reading through my newsfeed commenting on posts and checking in with my friends before I figure out what my plan is for the day.

Someone bangs on my door and I jump, afraid to answer it.

"Who is it?" I call.

"It's your mother, open this door right now."

I look up to the heavens and beg for strength because this woman doesn't get it. I count to ten before opening the door. When I finally do I find my mother standing there dressed in a pretty, fitted knee-length dress that probably ran her at least five hundred dollars. It's a gorgeous shade of green that matches her eyes.

"Come in, Mother." I turn my back to her and walk back into my apartment.

"Patricia, I know you're upset but ignoring me isn't going to fix our situation. Please talk to me, darling."

"Why? You don't listen to me. You continue to interfere in my life, trying to turn me into someone I'm not." With total frustration I plop myself onto my couch.

"Darling, I don't know what you're talking about. I'm only trying to do what I think is best for my only child."

"Mother, I'm turning twenty-five years old. I have a career, I support myself, and I have my own home. I do not need you managing my life. I can handle it all by myself."

"I guess I just don't understand why you won't give Ben another chance. He is such a good boy and wants to take care of you. He told me he tried to talk to you Saturday night and you wouldn't even hear him out."

"*Talk* to me?" I growl. "Mother, he practically yanked me out of the ballroom and into a secluded area, hurting my arm and embarrassing me. He probably would have hit me again if Carter hadn't come along and told him to screw off."

"I'm sure you must be overreacting," she says, lowering herself onto the edge of my chair like she really doesn't want to sit on it but doesn't want to be rude.

"Mother, I'm not overreacting. He was drunk, and I'm not sure why you support a cause like a battered woman's shelter when you're okay with a man like Ben hitting your own daughter."

"I'm not okay with him hitting you but he said he was sorry and promises me it will never happen again. He loves you, darling, and wants to propose. His family is very well off and I wouldn't have to worry about you if you married a man like him."

I shake my head. "First, I will *not* be marrying him. Second, I don't care if his family is the richest family in the world, I'm not giving him a second chance because I don't care about money the way you do."

"That's not fair. I love Richard," she says, turning her face like I've offended her.

"I'm sure you do, but you also love money. That's not me. I want to find a man who loves me for me. I would rather make my own money and find a man who truly loves me than marry someone who's rich and only wants me for arm candy. So, you have two choices, Mother. You can start accepting me for who I am and we can continue to have a relationship or you can continue feeding Ben false hope and pushing your lifestyle on me guaranteeing I will continue to push you away for good. What's it going to be?"

"I can't believe you're giving me an ultimatum." She has tears in her eyes and she's starting to make me feel bad, but I refuse to give in to her.

"I don't want to, Mother, but you're leaving me no choice. I'm not you and although I love you, I do not want to *be* you. You have to let me be me and live my life!"

"Fine," she huffs, "No more interfering. I still want you to make appearances at my events, though. It makes me look good and it's good for your books."

"Deal," I say with a small smile, hoping she means it.

"Good, because I have another event coming up in a few weeks and we'd really like for you to be there. Richard missed the last one because of a case, but he'll be at this one."

"Fine. Send me an e-mail with the info and I will make an appearance. I will also let my agent know that I'll be there so she can blab that her bestselling author will be at the event. She loves throwing my name out."

"Great. Now change out of those yoga pants because Bella will be here any minute to have lunch with us."

"Mom, just because I work from home doesn't mean you can simply drop in and interrupt my entire afternoon," I whine, because she does this to me often.

"You need to eat, darling. I promise a quick lunch and some shopping and I'll have you right back here so you can work. It's not like you can't work from home this evening."

"What if I have plans with Carter this evening?"

"Are you seeing that boy? You can do so much

better than that."

"Mom," I warn and she backs right off.

A few minutes later my buzzer rings and I let Bella in. She walks right in and air kisses my mom's cheeks before giving me a hug.

"Why are you in yoga pants?" she asks. "I thought we were going out?"

I raise one eyebrow at my mother. "We are but I only found out a minute ago. Luckily I've already showered and just need to change. I'll be back in a few minutes."

Bella turns to my mom giving her a questioning look.

My mom says, "Don't you start on me too."

After changing into some skinny jeans, a sweater, and some calf-high boots, I walk back out of my room with my hair in a ponytail, wrapping an infinity scarf around my neck. "Let's do this."

"Don't you look cute," Bella says.

"I can be cute when I want to. Just because I don't want to dress up like you two all the time doesn't mean I can't."

Bella laughs at my outburst. While I'm locking the door my mother is already heading downstairs to call her car around since she refuses to drive.

"Sometimes I swear you do it just to piss your mother off," Bella remarks.

I shrug. "Maybe if she didn't push it on me and let me be, I would do it more often, but I'm tired of her trying to turn me into someone I'm not and I told her so today."

"Fill me in later," she says as we are approaching my mother.

Mother's car pulls up and Phil gets out of the driver's seat to open the door for us. My mother and Bella climb in and he says, "Good afternoon, Ms. Patricia."

"Good afternoon, Phil. How are you?"

"I'm well," he says, tipping his head.

After I am inside he closes the door behind me and we're off to get lunch. He pulls up to one of my mother's clubs and we go inside. As always the door is opened for us and they tell my mom that our table is ready. I'm given a dirty look because I'm wearing jeans and a sweater, but they don't dare say anything because my stepfather spends a lot of money at this club.

Once we're seated my mother says to me, "Darling, my next event is being held here, so please be sure to dress appropriately."

I know she is only saying it because of the look I got at the door. "No problem, Mother. Had I been informed of our plans for the day perhaps I could have dressed appropriately."

"I know, dear, and I do apologize."

The menu is placed down and the hostess walks away after letting us know that Trevor is our waiter and he'll be right over. I open my menu, not wanting to carry on with the conversation that was just taking place because I really want to call her on it more. However, I decide to try to make the most of the remainder of my afternoon.

After a few moments of us quietly looking over the menu, Bella says, "So what are you ladies having?"

The tension must be killing her. "I'm going to

have chowder and salad," I reply.

"Nice choice," my mother says. "Luckily you can afford the calories of their delicious chowder. I, however, cannot, so I'm going to have a grilled salmon salad."

"I'm with you," Bella says, "The chowder is delicious but with a shoot coming up I can't do it. I think I'm going to have the grilled tuna."

After the waiter takes our order, my mother says, "So, darling, tell me about this next book you're writing."

Easy question, I think to myself, however, I'm not sure how I feel about the book so how much do I tell?

"It's about a woman who's approaching her thirties and has yet to find love. She's dated and has even been in a long term relationship but none that made her feel truly loved, so she starts to wonder what being in love is really like. When she finally meets Mr. Right she can't see it because she's such a mess over her past relationships. You know me, my characters have a mind of their own and the book could head in a totally different direction, but that was the idea."

"It sounds sweet," Bella says. "How far in are you?"

"Five chapters. It can really take a turn at any time, although for some reason I'm really having a hard time focusing with this one. I know I want her to have a happy ending, however, I can't seem to figure out how to make that happen for her."

"It will come to you, darling. Take your time and don't stress over it. Forget about that agent of yours.

You know there is no way she'll drop you because she makes money off your books."

"Very true. Why am I letting her rush me? It's not like they've given me an advance on the book yet. I'm going to take my time and I can worry about timing once she gives me my advance. As a matter of fact, if she keeps pushing me I may even push to change my contract on this one."

"There you go, that's my girl. Tell her you want more money for all the undue pressure."

I giggle at my mother's thoughts again heading in the direction of money. I make six figures a year off my books and if this one hits the bestsellers' list I'll be pretty well set.

Our food arrives, and we eat quickly so we can move onto shopping. My phone pings in my pocket and instantly I feel bad that I forgot to silence it.

"Excuse me," I say, taking it out to silence the ringer. I see there is a text from Carter.

Carter: Hope you're having a good day. I can't wait to see you tomorrow.

Patty: I'm at lunch with my mom and Bella and then we're going shopping. I'll fill you in tomorrow.

Carter: Call me later if you need to talk.

Patty: Thanks, will do!

I'll probably end up calling him later. We've spoken almost every night this week. He's been looking for an apartment now that he has a job and I know how tiring that can be. I make a mental note to ask him about it later.

"Sorry, that was Carter asking how my day was going." I put my phone back in my purse and finish my lunch.

When we're all finished my mom signs the bill. She and my stepfather are members here, and they have an account that gets charged each time they eat here. The driver brings the car around, and we all pile in. My mother tells us she's taking us to some fancy new dress shop she heard about to buy us dresses for her next event. Bella, being the girly one, claps her hands excitedly while I sit and enjoy the ride.

"I would like a black dress this time," I say as we're driving toward the shop.

"Why black, darling?"

"I like it and I think it's elegant and sexy." I don't dare tell her that I'm hoping to get Carter to attend with me and if I'm in black it will look good next to either a tux or his dress uniform. He wore a tux last time, though I'm not sure if that was out of choice or if he is not allowed to wear his dress uniform now that he is retired.

We pull up to the shop and I jump right out telling Phil not to worry about the door. My mother runs the poor man ragged. Bella and my mom follow behind me and Bella shuts the door. We walk into the shop and the girl behind the counter is drooling because she saw us get out of my mom's limo.

"How can I help you ladies this afternoon?"

105

"We need three formal, floor length dresses. My daughter Patricia wants black and Bella wants...?" She turns to Bella.

"Red, deep sexy red," Bella says with sass.

The woman tells us she will be right back and she returns in a matter of minutes. She's carrying three black dresses and two red ones. Bella and I go into fitting rooms to try them on. The first one I put on is pretty and I show my mom but it's not what I want. I go back in and when I come out, Bella is dancing around, thrilled with her dress. This time I'm a bit happier with what I'm wearing but I still want to try the third. I put on the last dress and when I come out I feel amazing. It's strapless with a low cut sweetheart neckline. It's fitted but the material is soft and gathers on one side, which flows down the length of the dress. It has some sort of black crystals throughout to make it sparkle and I love it.

My mom tells the woman she'll take them and then tells her she wants something that will compliment her eyes and her pale brown hair.

The woman says, "I know just the dress." She runs off to get it while we look at shoes. Bella and I have found shoes by the time she comes back with the dress. My mother is unsure with it on the hanger. We tell her to try it on anyway and when she comes out of the fitting room she is elated because it's beautiful. It's a simple floor length dress that's a deep shade of purple. It really makes her eyes pop and will look stunning next to my stepfather's black tux.

"I'll take all three, as well as the shoes they've

chosen," she tells the salesperson.

We find her shoes to match, and the girl packs up our purchases.

"Where are we off to next, ladies?" my mother questions.

"I need to get home," I say. "I told you lunch and a shopping trip. You have found our dresses for the next event, now I need to get home so I can work."

My mother pouts. "Phil, please head to drop Patricia off at her apartment."

"Yes, Ma'am."

As Phil is pulling up to my house I look at my watch and see it's already after three o'clock. I need to get some work done before Carter gets off so I can call him and catch up with him.

I thank my mom for lunch and the dress and climb out of the limo. Bella gets out with me and tells my mom she'll see her soon. We both wave as Phil pulls away.

"Okay, so what happened with you and your mom?"

I sigh. "I told her she either lets me live my life or she's not in my life. She chose to let me live my life."

"Wow. Did she freak out?"

"I wouldn't say she freaked out, but she wasn't happy. I'm tired of her pushing Ben on me. He pulled me out of the ballroom the other night, yanking on my arm and telling me he wanted to talk and I was going to listen. The only reason he didn't hurt me was because Carter showed up."

"I'm glad he did, Ben is such an ass."

"Oh, and speaking of Carter, I'm going to ask

him to go with me to the fundraiser just so you know."

She grins. "I figured as much."

She hugs me goodbye. "I'll let you get back to your writing. Keep me posted on how things are going with you guys and maybe we can do lunch again soon."

"Great! Love you, Bella!"

"Love you too!" she says and slides into her red sports car.

***

I spent the last few hours tweaking my book. I will send some more off to my agent tomorrow with a request for a meeting to discuss the direction of this book as well as when they're going to offer me a contract on it. While I am contemplating this, my phone rings. I grin when I see Carter's name across the screen and answer.

"Hey, big guy, how was your day?"

"It was all right. How'd lunch go?"

"I was about to jump in the shower. Could you call me back and I'll fill you in? Give me about twenty minutes."

"Does that mean you're standing in your bathroom naked right now?"

I giggle into the phone. "I'm about to be."

He moans. "Now that I'm picturing you naked, I guess I'll go take a shower too. Talk to you in twenty."

"Okay, Carter."

I quickly do what I have to do so I can get comfy

in time for him to call me back. After I'm showered and dressed I fix a bite to eat and just as I'm finishing up my phone rings again.

"Hey!"

"What are you doing?" he asks as I'm getting comfortable on the couch with one of my favorite blankets.

"I'm lying on the couch thinking about you. What are you doing?"

He laughs. "I'm lying on the couch thinking about you."

"No you're not." I say with laughter.

"I'm dead serious. I'm lying here thinking about what we should do for our date tomorrow night. Do you want to go out somewhere or do you want to hang home and order pizza?"

"Why don't you come here and we can order pizza and watch a movie, since we never got to the movie the other night."

"Deal. Now that that's settled do you want to tell me what happened with your mom or do you want to forget about it for now?"

"We can talk about that tomorrow, but I do want to ask if you'll go to one of her fundraisers with me in a few weeks."

"I'd love to go with you. Are you ready to face the media showing up with me again?"

"Shouldn't I be asking you that?"

"Not really, you're the one who has to deal with them."

"I don't know what to tell them," I say with a sigh.

"Tell them I'm your boyfriend. Unless you don't

want me to be your boyfriend," he says, sounding nervous and I think it's cute.

"No, I do, I guess I wasn't sure since we only went on one date. I don't want to scare you off already."

"It's going to take a lot more than some paparazzi to scare me away from a beautiful woman like you."

I blush, though he can't see it. "Thanks." It comes out in barely a whisper.

"You're welcome. How's the book coming?"

"It's coming. I'm going to make a few more changes tomorrow and then I'm emailing it off to my agent in hopes of meeting with her about a contract next week. How's the apartment hunting and the new job?"

"Both are great actually. My boss and I get along well, and I met with a veteran today to help him get some benefits. Also, I think I found an apartment."

"Sounds like a pretty productive day."

"It was. The apartment is perfect. It's a two bedroom, with a gorgeous kitchen. I don't cook, so I'm not sure what I'll do with such a nice kitchen, but whatever."

I start laughing. "Maybe once you're moved in I can give you some basic lessons."

"Are you serious? I'd love that. I wish my mom taught me how to cook, but instead she likes to take care of me, and would rather do it for me."

"Yeah, I'm serious. I can cook. I don't make gourmet meals or anything but I can hold my own."

"Great! I can't wait. I want to go furniture shopping this weekend, will you help me?"

"Sure, we can make set plans tomorrow."

"Thanks, well I'm going to get some sleep. I've been getting up really early so I can work out before work and I'm pretty beat."

"Okay, goodnight Carter."

"Good night, sweetie," he says as he cuts the call.

I can't help the huge smile that spreads across my face because he called me sweetie.

Chapter 10

Carter

"Holy shit!" I scream as the ground shakes. We all jump out of our trucks and take our positions attempting to assess what's going on around us. "Guys, take cover!" I shout as my men take off running. The shooting starts up again and it's fierce. Bullets are flying all around us as we try to get to our next destination. We're pinned down and not in the best situation, because there is not a lot of cover out here. I low crawl over to Seth and grab his radio.

"This is Staff Sergeant Montgomery, we're pinned down and taking on heavy fire! We need back up!"

"Ten-four, what's your location?"

"We're about five miles south of our destination. Do you copy?"

"We copy. Backup's on the way, hold tight."

We crawl into a position to try and take out our targets but we're heavily outnumbered until we get air support from above, and luckily for us it only *takes a matter of minutes. There are grenades dropping and bullets flying all around us.*

I sit up in bed soaked in sweat as I look over at the clock. Four-thirty. I get out of bed, panting as I throw on some clothes to hit the gym. I've got to do something about these nightmares.

I hit the elliptical hard for a good forty-five minutes straight, then start lifting. By the time I'm done it's almost six and I need to start getting ready for work. I feel so much better after that workout.

That's when I remember that I'm going to Patty's tonight for pizza and a movie and my entire day gets better. I shower and dress, then go to the kitchen for a quick breakfast.

When I get to my office, I find I'm the first one there and that's fine with me because I have a training session I'm supposed to complete today and a meeting with a veteran this morning. I boot up my laptop and log into my email to find I have a few emails that need answering. As I'm finishing up going through my emails Derek comes walking in.

"Good morning."

"Hey, man, Good morning."

"You okay? You look like you had a bad night."

I sigh. "I had another nightmare and I can't figure out why. It woke me at four-thirty. I got up to work out and then I came here."

"Same nightmare?" he asks me, full of concern.

"Pretty much. It was a close call attack we had in Iraq, though not the one that ended my career."

"Yeah, I bet as an MP you ran into a lot of close call attacks. Have you tried talking to someone about it?"

"No. I guess I may have to though, because I can't let them rule me. Although the flashbacks have gotten way better, the nightmares are coming a couple times a week."

"Try to figure out what triggers them and then maybe you can figure out how to avoid them. Anything bad happen last night?"

"No. As a matter of fact, I had a nice night. Patty and I talked on the phone as usual and we actually said we were going to officially announce us as a couple at a public event we will be attending together in a few weeks, and I'm seeing her for pizza and a movie tonight."

"Does she know?"

"Does she know what?"

"Does she know about your PTSD?" I shake my head. "You need to tell her."

"Wait, you think I had a nightmare because I haven't told her that I have PTSD?" I want to call bullshit, but can I? Was that really my head's way of reminding me that I haven't said anything to her yet? I know I should, but I don't want to scare her away either.

"Dude, I can tell you're thinking about it right now. You're not going to scare her away. Be honest and tell her before you scare the shit out of her in the middle of the night."

"We haven't even gone there yet."

"And you probably never will unless you tell her. Don't keep secrets, man. Not if you really like her."

"Thanks. I have to log on for a class now, so I'll

talk with you about it more another time," I say, trying to end our conversation.

Clearly he's not done. "I'm not letting this go. I'm going to help you through this," he says, shaking his head as he walks out the door.

I click the link I need to log into my class and then shut my office door so I'm not interrupted. I can't help but think about what Derek said as I wait for the class to start. How do I bring this up in conversation? *'Hey Patty, by the way I have horrible nightmares because of the war?'* I shake my head. I know Derek is right because if I have a nightmare and don't tell her I'm going to scare the shit out of her, and that's the last thing I want to do.

My screen comes alive and the instructor tells us it's time to start.

***

I'm just about done with my day when my office phone rings. It's my new landlord telling me I can pick up my keys since the checks for my deposit and first month's rent have cleared the bank. My month officially starts next week, but he's giving me the keys early, since I'm a vet and all. He also gave me a great discount, which I thought was pretty cool. I thank him and tell him I'll be moving in soon.

I send Patty a text.

Carter: Leaving work soon, is it cool if I head over?

Patty: Sure, but just so you know I decided to make us dinner instead.

Carter: That's cool, what are we having?

Patty: Chicken stir fry with brown rice. I hope that's ok?

Carter: It's perfect and way healthier than pizza.

Patty: Lol, see you soon.

I stop by Derek's office to let him know that I'm done for the day. When I get there he's hanging up the phone.

"Have a good night, man," I say.

"Have you thought about what I said?" he says, not dropping our conversation from before.

"I have and it makes sense. I guess I just don't know how to bring it up. It's not an everyday conversation."

He nods. "You're right, but you have to learn how to handle it. Who better to practice on than your girlfriend, right?"

"I guess. I'm going over there now. She's making me dinner and then we're going to watch a movie."

"Cool, have a great night."

"Yeah, you too."

I walk out the door so excited to see her. I can't wait to go pick up the keys to my apartment tomorrow so I can show it to her and then go pick some furniture out. I stop and buy her some fresh flowers on the way to the house assuming the old ones are dead. When I ring her buzzer she doesn't even ask who it is, she just buzzes me in. When she opens her door I have the flowers in front of my face and she bursts out laughing. I lower the bouquet to find her standing there in a cute pink fitted sweater and hip hugger jeans. I step in and give her a kiss. She wraps her arms around my neck and deepens it.

"How was your day?" she asks, breaking our kiss.

"It was a bit tiring, but seeing you has given me a fresh burst of energy."

"Good, come in. Dinner's almost ready. I bet that will help too."

"That's great, because I'm starving. I only got to eat part of my lunch today since I had a ton of emails when I got to work and then I had a class and a meeting."

I follow her into the kitchen and wrap my arms around her narrow waist. She turns in my arms.

"I can make you feel all better after I feed you."

"And I can't wait." I kiss her one more time and she slaps my arm playfully then shoves me away so she can finish dinner.

"Will you put those flowers in water for me? The vase is under the sink."

"Sure thing." I pull out the vase. "Where are some scissors that I can use to cut the bottoms?"

She turns around, grinning. "You know to cut the bottoms?" I shrug, not really knowing how I know that but I do. "They're in that drawer." She points with her chin.

"It smells amazing in here by the way."

"Thanks. It's chicken teriyaki with onions, peppers, snap peas, and pineapple. It's done, I just need a few more minutes for the rice and we can eat."

She's already set the table for us and it looks great. "Thank you so much for doing all of this."

"It's really no problem. I don't mind cooking, I just don't do it often because it's only me. Do you want beer or wine?"

"Beer, please." I finish putting her flowers in water.

She goes to the freezer for a mug and takes a beer from the fridge, pouring it into the frosty glass for me.

"Oh girl, you're going to spoil me if you keep this up."

"Says the man who's brought me flowers twice now." She looks at me with a grin on her face and I laugh. She takes the plates she has sitting on the counter and puts rice and chicken teriyaki on both, placing them on the table. I take the wine glass she has out and head to the fridge to fill it with wine for her while she finishes what she's doing. I walk over with my beer in one hand and her wine in the other and we sit to enjoy the meal she's made us.

I take a bite and my eyes go wide. Man this is good. My woman can really cook. I moan in appreciation. "Sweetie, this is delicious."

"Thank you, I'm glad you like it."

We both go into silence eating our dinner. Part of me starts to wonder if I should bring up my nightmares, but I don't want to ruin our dinner. When we're done eating I help her clear the table and clean up the mess so she isn't left to deal with it later.

"Oh, before I forget, I need to pick up the keys to my apartment tomorrow. Do you want to come with me so you can see it and then we can do lunch and go furniture shopping?"

"Yeah, that sounds great."

Damn, a yawn escapes me from lack of sleep last night and I'm really hoping she doesn't notice. I'm rinsing dishes and she's stacking them in the dishwasher. She takes the pans and nudges me away from the sink to wash them. I take my wet hands and flick water at her. She giggles and grabs the faucet sprayer like she's going to spray me and I give her a warning look.

"If you squirt me I will be forced to strip." She bites her lip and soaks my shirt with her hands. I burst out laughing, trying to get my hands wet again so I can splash her but she's flinging water at me. We're laughing hysterically when she nearly slips, but I catch her.

Panting out of breath I look deep into her eyes, placing my lips over hers. She opens to me and our tongues start exploring one another's. She moans into my mouth when my hand squeezes her delightfully round ass. Her hands start pulling at my shirt, attempting to untuck it from my jeans.

When I break our kiss she pants, "You're all wet." She giggles and it's the cutest sound I've ever heard.

"You're pretty wet yourself."

"In more ways than one," she says, blushing.

My lips collide with hers in a much more passionate kiss and I slide my hands up under her shirt, caressing her bare skin. She's wearing an off the shoulder shirt so her bra is strapless and I realize I can have it off in seconds. I kiss my way over to her ear and I nibble on her earlobe.

"You feel amazing pressed against my body, Patty."

"Carter, I want you, but I don't know if I'm ready."

"Sweetie, it's all right. We don't have to go there yet." I glide my tongue down her neck to her collarbone then kiss her again. "Can I take care of you?" She moans a yes and I pick her up and carry her to the couch where I know I'll have a bit more control. I lay her down then climb on top of her, pressing her into the couch. I slide my hand up under her shirt while I look into her eyes, watching for her reaction. I pull her strapless bra down to uncover her breasts and cup one, massaging it. I can see how affected she is and I can feel it as her hips grind into mine. Her eyes start to close.

"Leave them open. I want you looking into my eyes when I make you come."

Her eyes fly open and she blushes fiercely. My hand leaves her breast and slowly slides down her body to the button of her jeans. Once I have them undone, she lifts her sweet little ass and I slide them off. I lay back on top of her and lift the front of her pretty pink sweater to expose her hardened nipples. I take one in my mouth and slip my hand into her panties. My fingers find their way into her folds to discover just how wet she really is and we both moan at the same time.

"God, woman, you weren't kidding. You really are wet for me. Are you ready to come?"

She nods and her hips start grinding with the motion of my fingers rubbing on her hardened clit.

"Sometime soon, I'm going to eat this delicious pussy of yours until you scream my name."

"Carter, I'm going to come," she moans. I pinch her clit, sending her over the edge and she moans out my name one more time as I continue rubbing her clit while she rides out her orgasm.

"Oh my God, that was amazing," she says, panting below me.

"Oh baby, I want to take my sweet time learning, touching and kissing every inch of this body."

She grins up at me. "Yeah, well I think it's time I learn how to massage one of your muscles."

"Oh really?" I say with laughter because it's cute to hear her call my cock a muscle.

She pulls my shirt up and over my head and gasps. "You have the sexiest body I've ever seen!" She glides her hands up my arms, over my pecs and down my abs. Her hand makes its way to the button of my jeans and when she gets the button undone she slips her hand inside, finding my fully erect cock waiting for her.

"Holy shit, you're huge."

I burst out laughing at the look on her face. "I'll work you up to it, I promise." She pushes me off of her and I am now kneeling on the couch in front of her. She gently slides my pants and boxers down over my hips, my cock now level with her face and her eyes grow wide. She wraps her hand around it, I gasp at the jolt that shoots through my cock from her touch. She starts sliding her hand up and down my length slowly, experiencing every inch of it. She starts to move faster and then she tightens her grip.

"My god, Patty, you're going to make me come." I close my eyes, enjoying the feel of her hand on my cock when I flinch from the feeling of her lips wrapping around the mushroom tip. My eyes fly open and I take a sharp breath. "If you don't want me to come in your mouth you need to stop because this feels so good I can't hold on." She starts sucking me deeper and as she does I lose control and start pumping my seed into her mouth. Her tongue glides over the tip ensuring she gets every last drop.

She pulls away looking at me dead serious and says, "How was that for a massage?"

"Sweetie, that was the best damn massage I've ever had." I lean down to kiss her. I mean it to be a sweet, soft kiss, but she pokes her tongue out begging for more, so I glide my tongue along hers and for the first time I can taste my release on another woman and she still tastes mighty fine.

"Sweetie, we start this again and I'm going to end up hard as a rock and I'm not sure I'll be able to control myself."

"I'm sorry, it's just I haven't felt this good in a long time."

"Trust me, I plan on sticking around to make you feel a lot more than that." I put my cock back in my pants and pull my shirt back on. She climbs off the couch and tells me she'll be back because she's going to change into a pair of more comfy pants. She bends over to pick up her jeans and literally strolls off to her room wearing a pink sweater and panties. I watch until I can't see her anymore. Fuck me. I'm hard all over again.

She comes back out in a pair of leggings and a t-shirt. The yawn I've been fighting escapes me, so I get up to meet her.

"Sweetie, I know I said we'd watch a movie, but I'm going to get going. I'm really sorry. I didn't sleep too well last night, and I'm pretty tired." I run my knuckles across her cheek, tucking her hair behind her ear. "I'll pick you up tomorrow around eleven?" I question as I slip my hand into her hair.

"Works for me. I had fun, thanks for coming over."

"Thanks for dinner."

I kiss her one more time and then head out the door.

Chapter 11

Carter

I wake Saturday morning and I feel pretty good. I slept restlessly, but I feel like I was able to keep the demons at bay. I stretch in bed before getting up to hit my home gym. I've started a good routine and I don't want to mess it up now. I know having a routine is going to help me deal with my issues, I just have to keep at it. I jump out of bed, throw on my gym clothes, and head downstairs to start on the elliptical, weights, and then practice my martial arts. I'm done working out in a little over an hour and when I get back upstairs I find my mom busy in the kitchen.

"Good morning, Mom. What are you doing up already?"

"It's eight in the morning, Carter, it isn't that early. How was your workout?"

"It was good. I'm going to go take a shower and then I'll come get some coffee."

"Okay, how about some breakfast?"

"Sure, Mom, that would be great." I run up the stairs to shower and dress in some jeans and a long sleeve shirt. I want to look good for Patty because I know she'll look cute as hell. I shave before getting in the shower to wash away the sweat of my workout.

While I'm washing, my mind drifts to last night when she was pressed into her couch by the weight of my body. God she felt good beneath me.

My thoughts are interrupted by a knock on the door, "Yeah!"

"Your breakfast is ready," my mother says through the door.

I love her dearly but this is why I need my own apartment, because she thinks I'm still in school.

"Thanks, Mom, be down in a second." I sigh as I rinse the soap from my body and shut off the water, dry off, and get dressed.

I'll miss my mom and it's nice having her prepare meals for me but I need some space. I'll have to have Patty start giving me cooking lessons so that I can continue to eat healthy in my own place. I'm hoping to be moved in soon, but right now all I have are the clothes in my room. Luckily for me I saved a ton of money while I was in the service.

I'm now fully dressed and ready to start my day. Hanging my towel on a hook, I open the door and run down for breakfast.

My mom has eggs, bacon, toast, and home fries set out on the table for me with coffee and juice.

My father comes in behind me. "Is he special or is there some for me too?"

My mother giggles and my dad grabs her for a kiss. "There's plenty for you too, darling. Have a seat and I'll bring some over."

"What are you up to today, son?" my dad asks.

"I'm picking up the keys to my new place and then I'm going to show it to Patty. We're having lunch and then she's going to help me pick out some furniture."

"Ah, so you and the princess have hit it off, huh?" I love that my father and are close enough that he's comfortable busting my chops.

"Yeah, I guess we have. You were right, she's way more like her dad than her mom. As a matter of fact, she and her mother had it out yesterday. We were supposed to talk about it, but I guess we both forgot."

"I hate to say it, but her mother is one tough cookie. She has been trying to change that girl her entire life. That's one of the biggest battles between Troy and Sandra. He really wants Sandra to leave Patty be, but she insists that Patty's place is on the arm of a rich man because she's the daughter of Sandra Fitzgerald-Carmichael."

"I keep forgetting she isn't Fitzgerald anymore. That's probably why she hates me so much. I keep referring to her as Fitzgerald."

My father laughs. "No, she hates you because you're not snobby and we don't flaunt our money. She swears she loves Richard, but I truly think she left Troy because he didn't have Richard's money. After all, he only owns the most dealerships of any one man in this part of the country. Although Richard's a district attorney, he comes from family money, and Troy had to work hard for his."

"You would think that would make her proud." I'm floored at this woman's behavior.

"I agree with you, son, but that isn't how she thinks. I also don't think Patty knows any of this. Their divorce was never really talked about."

My mother places my father's plate in front of him full of fresh food. "That woman drives me crazy," she says. "We were friends at one point in life, but now I only tolerate her because we need to stay in the good graces of the media for business purposes."

"I know, Mom. You have to play nice because in this world if you cause issues customers will pull out, and it's hard to walk the line of playing nice and being fake." I push my empty plate away and sip my coffee, looking at my watch. "Listen, I'll probably be gone most of the day and I think I'm going to take Patty for dinner, so don't expect me home until late." I stand to rinse my cup and dish, placing them in the dishwasher.

I kiss my mom on the cheek and thank her again for a delicious breakfast, then run upstairs to grab a jacket, my cellphone, and put my wallet in my back pocket. Before I head out the door I send Patty a text because I'm going to be a bit early and I want to make sure she's okay with that.

Carter: Was going to head over. Is that ok?

Patty: Sure, I'm ready for you.

Carter: Great, see you soon.

I slip my phone into the clip on my belt and go back downstairs. I shake my father's hand and tell him I'll see him later then I'm out the door to go see my girl. I drive straight to her house, excited to see her. I don't think I've ever been so excited to see a girl, but her smile and her beautiful hazel eyes make me so happy.

I park in front of her place and run up to push the buzzer. She buzzes me in immediately like she was waiting for me and it makes me smile. When I get to her door, it's already open. Upon entering I find her sitting on the couch with several wrapped boxes.

"What's that?" I ask her.

"It's a housewarming gift for your apartment. I went and did some shopping this morning," she says with a shy smile.

"That's so nice of you. You didn't have to do that." I close the door and take a seat next to her.

"I know I didn't have to, I wanted to. Here open this one first," she says, handing me a box.

I rip open the paper and find a really nice pot and pan set. "You got me cookware." I grin.

"Yup, so I can teach you how to cook," she says so proudly.

I lean over to kiss her. "Thank you so much, that was very sweet of you."

"Here there are two more." She pushes another box toward me and again I rip the paper off. This time I open a box of nice dishes. She has picked a set that is nice, but masculine too.

"Are these for us to eat the meals you're going to teach me to cook on?"

"You got it."

I laugh as she pushes the last box toward me. Once I start pulling the paper off I see a set of glasses and again I laugh. "Drinks to go with dinner?"

She nods and giggles at my excitement.

"I love it all, thank you so much." I place my finger under her chin and pull her toward me, "You look gorgeous today," I say, placing another kiss on her lips.

"Thanks. You look pretty hot yourself."

"Are you ready to go see my new place?"

"Let me get my jacket." She walks off to her room, and when she gets back a minute later she's slipping on her coat. She picks up the smallest box while I grab the larger two and we head out the door to load them into my Jeep.

"What do you need for furniture?" she asks when we're in the Jeep and buckled in.

"Everything. I left my parents' house to join the Army and when I got out on my medical discharge I went back to their house, so I have nothing."

"I guess we have a bit of shopping to do then, don't we?"

About fifteen minutes later we pull up to my new place. I haven't said this to her, but I'm secretly happy that my place isn't too far from hers. We get out of the car and walk up to the front door.

The doorman opens it for us. "Hello, Mr. Montgomery, it's nice to see you again."

"Thank you. This is my girlfriend, Patty, please be sure she gets let up to my place with no problems."

He nods. "How do you do, ma'am?"

She nods back. "I'm well, thank you."

We go inside and over to the front desk where the building manager is waiting for me. I introduce Patty to the manager and he walks us over to the elevator to go up to my new apartment. I like this place because there are only two apartments on my floor, mine and one across the hall from me.

The landlord opens the door and we walk into my huge new living room which has hardwood floors and a gas fireplace. The kitchen is to the right and it's huge with a massive snack bar. It has all state of the art appliances, brown granite countertops, and darker brown wood cabinets. There is a short hall that has two bedrooms at the end of it. One will be for workout equipment and one will be for me to sleep. My master bedroom has a huge walk in closet and its own bathroom with a garden tub, shower, and his and her sinks.

"Carter, this place is gorgeous," she says as she wanders around checking out every inch of the place.

The manager asks, "Do you have any questions?" I shake my head. He hands me my keys. "Welcome to the building. Let us know if you have any questions or problems."

"Will do, thanks." I shake his hand and he walks out the door, leaving us to ourselves. I walk over to Patty and wrap my arms around her. "Do you like it?"

"I think it's great! Do you have any idea what you want for furniture?"

"I think something masculine, but nice and

cozy."

"Like a black leather sofa and loveseat maybe?"

"Maybe, I would have to see it. Why don't we hit the furniture store up the street? They have furniture for every room. I'll order my workout stuff online."

"Sure," she says and we head out the door.

***

Three hours later, we have chosen furniture for both the living room and my bedroom. For the living room we went with a nice black sofa with gray loveseat and chair. Patty convinced me to get a gray and white area rug and a nice black coffee table for accents. The top elevates to expose storage space, and also becomes a TV tray if we want to enjoy dinner while watching a movie.

For my bedroom, I went with a king size bed. All the furniture is a deep, rich brown. Although I didn't find a dining set I liked, we did pick a set of six stools for the snack bar so we can eat there too if we want.

After hours of shopping we choose to eat at a nice Italian place nearby. When we pull up to the restaurant the place is rather quiet because it's past lunchtime, though too early for dinner. We're seated right away.

"Will you help me set my place up when my furniture is delivered?" I ask Patty.

"Of course I will. I can't believe it's all going to be delivered on Friday. As a matter of fact, if you like I can be at the apartment to accept the delivery while you're at work. I'll bring my laptop over and work from there."

"Are you sure? That would be awesome, because then I can ask to leave early instead of taking the whole day. They aren't supposed to be there until three, but if they come early I'd be screwed if I wasn't home."

"I don't mind at all. Just leave when you can and we'll do dinner and set things up when you get home."

"Thank you so much, Patty, that's a huge help."

Our waitress comes over and asks if we are ready to order.

"Lunch size chicken parm please," Patty requests.

"And you, sir?" the waitress asks.

"Spaghetti and meatballs please."

She collects our menus, smiles, and walks away.

"How are your mom and dad?" Patty asks.

"I think my mom is bummed I'm moving out. She was up this morning and made me a big breakfast. I love her and appreciate her, but she forgets how old I am and that I need my space."

"Yeah, that can be tough. Does your mom work? Maybe she needs something to do."

"No. She should though because I think you're right, she needs something to occupy her time. She was working in my dad's office for a while but stopped when I came home so she could help me, and she never went back. Speaking of parents, what happened with you and your mom?"

She sighs deeply. "She pissed me off going on and on about Ben. I hung up on her and wouldn't answer her calls. Then she showed up at my house to discuss the situation with me and I gave her an ultimatum. I told her that she either lets me live my life for me or she gets out of it. She wasn't happy, but decided to leave me alone about it."

"Wow, I'm quite proud of you for sticking up for yourself with her. I'm sure it wasn't easy."

"No, it wasn't. To be honest, I'm not sure I believe it will be the last of the discussion. If it gives me a little peace, then that's fine for now. She kills me though. She thinks because she bought me a dress for that event that means all is okay with us, and that there's nothing more she needs to do. In reality she needs to show me that she's really going to change and stop interfering in my life."

Our waitress comes back with our food and tells us to enjoy. We chat lightly while we eat, planning to go to more stores when we're done. I still need bedding, bathroom essentials, eating utensils, and I'm sure so much more. As we're finishing eating I get a text from my dad.

Dad: Mom bought you a ton of towels for your bathroom and for your kitchen.

Carter: Tell her I said thanks, she didn't have to do that though.

Dad: She wanted to do something to help with your apartment.

Carter: Patty got me some stuff too.

Dad: Nice.

Carter: We're finishing lunch and then we're off to buy some bedding and stuff.

Dad: Talk to you later.

"That was my dad," I said to Patty when I put my phone away. "He was letting me know that my mom bought me a bunch of towels and stuff for the bathroom."

"Aww, that's sweet. I feel like I haven't seen your parents in years."

The waitress comes back over and I ask for the bill with my credit card in hand. She shows it to me and I hand my card right over to her so we can get out of here.

"Maybe we should plan a dinner at my place with both our parents so I can show my parents my apartment and get everyone together," I suggest when the waitress walks away.

A look of concern flashes across Patty's face though it's gone in a second. "Sure, that sounds great."

"What's wrong, Patty?"

"I guess I'm just not sure I want to have my father at the house at the same time as my mother. I think I would just want to have my father since he's friends with your parents, though I feel like if my mother found out she'd be mad."

The waitress comes back with the slip. I sign it and slide out of the booth, grabbing Patty's hand to pull her after me.

"We can talk about it later and we'll do it however you're comfortable."

We get in the car and prepare to leave. She sighs and I can tell she's thinking about it as she looks out the window. It makes me feel bad that she's in this situation although, to be honest, since my parents don't get along with her mother that well I'm just as happy to have just her father over. We're both sitting in complete silence as we drive toward the store.

I don't know what to say to turn her mood around. I'm glad the store isn't far because this will at least occupy her. I pull into the parking lot of the next store and place my hand on Patty's knee, giving her a gentle squeeze. When she looks over to me I ask, "Are you all right?"

"Yeah, I'm just trying to figure out the best way to manage this situation. I know how my mother is and I'm sure that your parents aren't friends with her since she divorced my father."

"They're not, but I'm sure they can play nice for one night."

"They shouldn't have to. They do it enough out in public at social events that cause them to intermingle. We don't need to add to it. We'll have your parents and my father over and figure something out another night with my mom."

"Are you sure? I don't want you to feel like we have to do it that way." I know my parents would play nice with her mom even though my mother can't stand her money hungry ways.

"Yes, I'm sure. Now let's go shopping."

135

Chapter 12

Patty

My phone buzzing on my nightstand wakes me. I look at my clock and see it's eight am and I'm wondering who the hell is calling me so early in the morning. Then I see it's Carter. We took a selfie in his empty apartment the other day and I made it his contact picture on my phone.

"Good morning," I answer sleepily.

"Good morning, sweetie, did I wake you?"

"Yeah, but I need to get my ass in gear because I have a meeting with my agent today to discuss the new book."

"I know, that's why I was calling. I wanted to wish you luck with your meeting."

"Thanks. How's your morning going?"

"Good. I'm sitting in my office going through emails missing my girl."

"I know, I'm sorry we haven't gotten together in a few days but I really wanted to focus on the book. I'm emailing my agent another chapter this morning to talk over at the meeting. I still have a long way to go but at least they have a good starting point."

"How about you call me after your meeting? If all goes well today we can go to dinner to celebrate."

"That sounds nice. I really miss you too, Carter. You teasing me Sunday night left me with good dreams, but it's also left me missing you."

He laughs into the phone. "I haven't slept too well since then either. Maybe I can make it up to you tonight."

"Oh yeah? What are you thinking?" I grin, flirting with my man.

"I'm thinking maybe I spend the night at your house, if you're okay with that."

"Are you serious?" I shoot straight up in bed. We've yet to spend the night together.

"I'm dead serious."

"I'm *so* okay with that. I can't wait to see you tonight."

"Okay, well I want to run one more thing by you and then I have to get back to work. I was thinking we would have your friend Bella and my friend Derek over with your mom the weekend after the fundraising event so that we can spend some time with them and have your mom over too."

"That would be great. Bella is close to my mom and it will be nice to have us all there together. I'll call Bella and talk to her and then I'll call my dad to talk to him about Saturday. Have you spoken to your parents?"

"Yes I have, and that would be great because my parents are coming so even if your dad can't we'll have dinner with them. Derek's walking in now. I'm going to let you go so I can talk to him about it."

"Okay, have a good day, Carter."

"You too. Let me know how it goes today."

I hang up with Carter and start to think about how much I really like him. What scares me is I like him a *lot,* and we've been spending a lot of time together, but how much do I really know him? I don't even know basic things like his favorite movie or band, what color he likes, or his favorite dishes. What if he spends the night tonight and snores like crazy keeping me awake? I sigh. I need to talk to Bella.

Patty: Are you awake?

Bella: Yup.

Patty: Can I call you?

My phone rings a second later.

"Hey girl!" I answer.

"You know you don't need to ask permission to call me, Patty. You're pretty much my sister."

"I know, but what if you were at a shoot or something? I know you said you have one coming up."

"I'm getting ready for a shoot now."

"What are you doing tomorrow? Want to do lunch?"

"Sure, what's up?"

"I'm meeting with my agent today. I'm hoping it

goes well and I'll get to do some celebrating afterward. I want to go to the salon to get a haircut for the new headshots."

"Hold on one second," she says to me. "Hey, Kelly, are you on a shoot tomorrow?" Bella calls out. Someone mumbles a response, then Bella comes back to the line. "Get your hair done first thing in the morning and then Kelly is going to meet us to do your pictures."

"Thanks, Bella, I didn't call you so you could arrange my shoot for me but I appreciate it."

"I know you didn't but I don't want you to keep pushing it off either. Just let me know what time your appointment is and I'll meet you then we'll go for pictures. We can have lunch and maybe some shopping after if you want."

"Great. Thanks again, Bella."

"No problem, girl! See you tomorrow and good luck today."

"Thanks."

I decide to text my dad instead of calling him because I have to get moving.

Patty: Hey Dad, I'm helping Carter move into his new apartment and we're having his parents over for dinner Saturday, are you free?

Daddy: For you of course I am.

Patty: Great see you at six.

Daddy: Looking forward to it.

I go into the kitchen for a cup of coffee, and call the salon. After making my appointment I send Bella a message letting her know that my appointment is at ten am. I've already laid out my outfit for my meeting, and once I have my coffee in hand I head for the shower to begin the process of turning Patty into P. A. Fitzgerald, bestselling author.

***

I walk into my agent's office wearing a black pencil skirt with a red button down shirt and a black jacket. I wore my black patent leather heels to top off the outfit. I don't usually dress this nice but I want to show I'm a professional and that I mean business. They say red is the color of power, so maybe it will help me get what I want. I'm going to work into my contract that I must have at least six months of uninterrupted time off before I will consider starting my next book, which actually means I won't get time off for a while. When I'm done writing, there's still creating the cover, editing and tweaking the book, cover reveals, book promoting, and then signings afterward.

"Good afternoon, Ms. Fitzgerald," the receptionist says. "Joan is ready for you. Go right in."

"Thank you." I walk toward Joan's office with my leather portfolio in hand, ready to negotiate.

When I walk through her door, she rises from her seat and practically runs up to me, hugging me and air kissing my cheek. Joan hasn't been with this agency long and I think she's busting my chops about another book because so far I'm her only bestseller for the company.

"Patricia, how are you?"

"I'm well, Joan, how are you?"

"Oh you know me, busy, busy all the time," she says with a smile. "Come take a seat. I saw the last chapter that you sent me and I have to say we love what you're writing. There's so much emotion and people are really going to connect with your characters."

"I'm glad you're happy with it. I have a long way to go, but now that you know what I'm writing we need to talk business. I have certain things I want written into this contract."

"Like what, darling?" she says in her snobbiest voice and it reminds me of my mother.

"Like an uninterrupted eight months off after the book releases and I do three signings." I figure she's going to talk me down so I'll start high and see what she says.

"Eight months, that's a long time."

"I need it. I'm starting a relationship and I want some time to myself to see where it goes and maybe do some traveling with my mother and Bella."

"I know I can get you six, though I'm not sure the agency will go for eight. How about if we do five signings after the release and six months?" she counteroffers.

I shake my head. "Listen, when I first started writing for you I was doing one book at a time and it was no big deal if I took time off in between books. Now that I'm a bestseller you're pushing me

141

for more. I get that this is a business, but these are my books and I won't be pressured to write. Five signings and eight months off or I self-publish this one." I stare her in the eyes and add, "You do realize I don't need to give you this book, right? Although I've fulfilled my last contract with you, I like the work you do for me and I'd rather not self-publish. That being said, if you cannot give me time off then I walk and I can have the control I need over my own career."

"Okay, I'll write it up and get it over to you once it's been signed off on. Be sure to keep promoting online and showing your face in the media. I'd also like for you to come up with a blurb for the book soon, something we can talk about. *'P.A. Fitzgerald's WIP—After years of bad relationship she finally finds her Mr. Right, but will she realize it too late?'* Whatever, just get me something."

I can't believe she didn't even try to talk me down. I really only wanted six, but I managed to get two more months out of her. Now I can start writing after about six or seven months off and surprise her with some work right at the eight month mark. I jot down a note to work on that blurb for her this week. Then I write down what she said because it's pretty good and I'll probably work with it.

"That was a pretty good blurb right there. Let me put some more thought into it and I'll get you something soon."

I stand to leave, shaking her hand. "Get me the contract. You'll see no more of this book or its blurb until I have it." I step toward the door. When I turn to tell her to have a good day, she has a look of complete shock on her face and I feel great. "Good day, Joan."

I walk out the door with my head held high and super proud of myself. I practically run to my car to call Carter because I can't believe I just handled the meeting the way I did. I'm usually so shy and just go with what they say. I'm done doing that. I need to start sticking up for myself and putting out there what I want. *I'm* the author. I should be able to do things at my pace. They are making a ton of money off my last few books so if I want time off damn it, I'm taking it.

I dial Carter's number and he answers instantly, like he's been waiting for my call. "Give me good news, sweetie."

"Although I'm waiting for the contract to come through to me, I told my agent I want eight months off and that I will do no more than five signings after the book release. We will see if she can come through, but I'm proud that I stood my ground with that part of it. I'm fine with the rest of my contract. I just don't want them driving me crazy while I'm taking time off after the book."

"That's great! Are we on for dinner tonight?"

"For sure. Why don't I cook and we can just relax at my place."

"That works under one condition."

"Are we negotiating a contract?"

He bursts into laughter. "No, but I want you to teach me how to cook. I was going to say you have to wait for me to get there so we can cook together."

"That sounds like fun. What time are you leaving work and what do you want for dinner?"

"I'm leaving here at four and I don't care what we have for dinner. Whatever you feel like making is fine."

"Okay, we'll make something easy. Oh, and my dad is all set for Saturday. I'm thinking about doing a large roast with potatoes and vegetables to make it easy."

"Sounds good, I'll see you in a little bit."

After I hang up with him, I go to the grocery store to get some things for dinner tonight. I'm going to show him how to make baked ziti with meat sauce. We both like pasta and it's really easy to make. I'll need to pick up some ingredients and garlic bread to go with it, as well as a bottle of wine to top off dinner.

A short time later I've managed to change into more comfortable clothes, tidy up my place, and set the table. Just as I'm about to pour myself a glass of wine my buzzer rings and I know it's Carter. I go over to press the button, letting him in, then open the door.

"Hey, pretty lady," he says, placing his warm, soft lips over mine.

"Hey yourself. How was your day?"

"Long. I'd ask how yours was, but I'm pretty sure it was a good day, huh?"

I smile. "And it just got even better." I take his hand and lead him to my bedroom so he can put his overnight bag in there.

"What's this?" he asks, seeing that I have some ingredients already laid out on the counter. I tell him the first thing we need to do to make dinner is chop onions and cook the meat. He goes to the sink to wash his hands and we get started on making dinner.

About twenty minutes later our ziti is in a baking dish and placed in the oven. I get Carter a beer in a frosted glass and refresh my wine. While we wait for the ziti to bake I tell him about my plans for tomorrow with Bella. "What's your favorite color?" I ask him out of the blue.

He wrinkles his brows. "What?"

"What's your favorite color?"

"Blue, why?"

I blush slightly, worried he'll think I'm silly. "I was lying in bed this morning thinking how much I've come to enjoy spending time with you and I realized that I like you a lot, then it dawned on me that I don't know a lot about you. Like your favorite color? Do you like movies or TV? We've tried to watch movies twice and didn't get to. Do you have a favorite dish? Silly things like that."

He approaches with a sense of purpose and places his fingers gently under my chin, lifting it so I'm forced to look into his eyes. "We have time to learn those things. I'm not going anywhere. To make you feel better, my favorite color is blue, I like both TV and movies, I love all food, and I do try to eat healthy, although it's not always easy."

I smile as he rambles off the answers to my questions.

The oven buzzes to tell us our dinner's ready, putting a stop to our conversation.

"Mmm, that smells so good," he says when I open the oven door.

"You made it," I say, smiling up at him.

I pull it from the oven and notice the garlic bread is done as well. I place the ziti on one side of the stove and the garlic bread on the other.

I scoop some ziti onto plates while he slices the garlic bread and we sit down to eat. It's already starting to get late and he has to work tomorrow morning.

"Will you stay with me at my place Friday night?" he asks.

"I'd love to. Then we can spend Saturday together tidying up the apartment before our parents get there. We'll need to do some grocery shopping Friday night though."

"We can go after work to stock my place with food, but you'll know better what to buy than I will. I just need to make sure I have some easier things on hand for when you're not there."

He takes his first bite and says, "Damn, I make a fine baked ziti," and winks at me.

I giggle as I take my first bite and we settle into a comfortable silence, eating our dinner. When we're done, I get up from the table, taking both our plates and rinse them off to put into the dishwasher. Carter comes up behind me, wrapping his arms around me and pressing his body into mine. He leans into my hair, taking a deep breath. "You smell heavenly," he says. "Thanks for the cooking lesson. That was fun."

"Help me clean up and we can move on to some more fun." I can't wait to feel his hands on my body.

He moves my hair to one side and kisses below my ear. "I can't wait to touch you," he says, sliding his hands over my hips to my ass, and he gives it a quick squeeze. Leaving me breathless he walks away to take care of the leftover bread. I groan in frustration because he is such a damn tease.

"There are containers up in that cabinet. Take down two and I'll pack some of this up for you to take home with you. There's no way I'll eat it all."

He slips behind me, grinding his cock against my ass while he reaches for the cabinet door. He gets the two containers out and I pack up the ziti to place it in the fridge. When I bend over in the fridge to put the food away he comes up behind me, rubbing his hands all over my ass. I stand to give him a look that screams '*really?*' but he just laughs. We need to move on to better things, but I still have the baking dish to clean. While I start doing so, Carter comes up behind me again and starts fondling my nipples through my thin bra. I groan out of frustration because he keeps teasing me.

He leans in to whisper in my ear, "Don't growl at me, I'll give you what you need, I promise." He nips on my earlobe, sending goosebumps all over my body.

I decide two can play at this game, so I start rubbing my ass against his cock hoping I'm teasing him as much as he is me.

When I'm finally done I turn around and he's right there with one hand on either side of me. He steps toward me, pinning me between him and the counter. His mouth crashes down on mine and our tongues collide into a heated kiss. I grab his ass and pull him even closer so I can feel his erection rubbing against my belly. I rub it through his jeans and he places a hand over mine to stop me.

"Bed," he orders. "I want dessert."

I bite my lip as he moves one of his arms, freeing me to lead the way.

He follows me and as soon as we're at the foot of my bed he slips his hand in mine and tugs gently to stop me from going any further. He slides my shirt over my head, unclips my bra, and slips the thin pink straps down my arms, exposing my breasts. He reaches around me, sliding his hand slowly up my stomach and over my right breast. He massages it for a second then pinches my nipple and it hardens further. He switches hands again, sliding up my stomach to my left breast, massaging it, and pinching my nipple. He walks around me and lowers his mouth, pressing his soft lips to mine. He stays like that for a bit, then he sticks his tongue out and caresses my lips with it. He pulls away as he slips his hands into the waistband of both my panties and leggings, sliding them down over my hips. He squats, taking them all the way down to my ankles, kissing various spots on my body along the way. I step out of each leg and he tosses them aside. He stands up and takes a few steps back to admire the view in front of him. A blush instantly creeps up as I shyly watch his eyes rake over my body. My eyes go to the floor as I can no longer stand him staring at me.

"Patty, you're beautiful. Please don't look at the floor. I want to see you."

I look up at him and lick my lips. "Somebody has far too much clothing on." I step towards him, pulling his shirt over his head exposing his muscular chest, and toss it off to the side with my leggings. My hands glide down his chest to the button of his jeans. I make quick work of it, releasing his massive cock. I still can't believe he's going to fit inside me but I guess we're about to see. I kiss his nipple, placing a trail of kisses down over his abs at the same time I slip his pants and boxer briefs down. He kicks his shoes off then finishes removing his pants and asks me to lie on the bed.

I lay down in the middle of my bed and he wastes no time. He kisses up the inside of my leg and when he gets to the top he buries his face in my pussy, lapping up every drop of the wetness he has created. His tongue finds its way through my folds to my clit and I moan at the pleasure. He starts licking me like I'm a feast and he hasn't eaten in days. My hips are moving and I couldn't stop them if I wanted to. I'm grinding against his face, as I'm about to come he shoves his tongue deep inside me and I explode all over it. I ride out my orgasm screaming his name as he fucks me with it. He's moaning, lapping up every drop. He kisses up my hip across my stomach to my breast where he sucks my nipple into his mouth. I moan again, loving the feeling of his lips and hands on my body.

He gets up for a condom, slipping it on then climbing back on top of me. He hovers over me for a minute looking deep into my eyes. "You know I really care about you, right? I mean like a lot."

I bite my lip and nod. "That's good, because I care about you too and I mean like a lot," I steal his words.

He smiles and lowers to kiss me. I can taste my

149

release, but I don't care. I want to be close to him. He deepens the kiss, slipping the head of his cock into my wet pussy. He's teasing my opening, trying to stretch me because it's been so long.

"Just give it to me," I say.

"Please be patient, I don't want to hurt you," he says, sliding his length deeper inside me.

I'm grinding my hips with him trying to get him to give it all to me, but he won't do it. "Carter, give it to me, I won't break."

He moves a little deeper but when he pulls it out this time he slams himself balls deep inside me and I whimper at the full feeling.

"Are you all right?"

I nod. "I'm fine, please, Carter."

He starts moving again so that he's giving me all he has. I wrap my legs around his waist as he's pumping his full length deep inside me. "Carter, I'm going to come."

"Give it to me, sweetie," he says. He slams into me a few more times and I explode into another incredible orgasm. My pussy tightens around his cock, milking him for his seed. He slams into me one last time, emptying himself deep inside me.

He collapses on top of me, panting from our little sexcapade.

"That was amazing, Carter," I say, attempting to steady my breathing.

He looks deep into my eyes and says, "That was definitely the best I've ever had."

I grin. "Let me clean up so we can get some sleep."

When I am in my bathroom he knocks on the

door.

"Come in."

I'm standing naked in front of the sink about to brush my teeth. He throws the condom in the trash and has a brand new toothbrush in his hand.

"Do you mind if I leave this one here?"

I shake my head.

He opens it and begins brushing his teeth alongside me. When we're done we get into bed and he spoons me from behind.

He kisses my head. "Sleep well, sweetie."

Chapter 13

Patty

I've been up for a while now. Carter slept in a bit this morning since I don't have a gym for him to work out in. He joked about us spending more time at his place so he can continue to work out on a regular basis.

I'm a bit sore from our night together and decide I need to stretch. I've already spent some time posting on social media, promoting the upcoming fundraising event that I'm attending to feed the hungry for the holidays, and talking about my new WIP. When I was done with that, I went online to look at some potential styles for my new haircut. I promised Carter I wouldn't cut it too short because he really likes my hair long.

It was such a nice night and I loved him holding me while we slept. He woke me this morning with the softest of kisses on my neck and cheek. He told me he couldn't wait to see me again tomorrow when we'd stay in his new apartment for the first night. I really think he wants to christen his new room, but hey, if it's anything like last night, I'm perfectly fine with that.

I'm jarred from my thoughts when the doorbell rings. I buzz Bella in. She comes up and I already have my purse and coat by the door. I can't believe how cold it's getting. Although I love the scenery at this time of year I hate having to bundle up.

"You could've just called me and I would've come down, Bella."

"It's no big deal. I'm parked right out front. Are you ready?"

"Yup, how do I look?"

"Your outfit is cute. We're meeting Kelly at her studio when you're done with your haircut."

"Thanks for setting that up for me."

"It's no problem, Kelly owes me. This shoot is on her."

"Even better," I say as I fold myself into her sports car. As soon as we're both in and buckled, she flies off in the direction of the salon. I bring up dinner at Carter's in a few weeks. "The weekend after the feed the hungry fundraiser Carter wants to have you and Mom over to his new apartment with his friend Derek. Is that cool?"

"Sounds good to me. What about your dad?"

"We're having his parents and my dad over on Saturday night for dinner. Because my mom is the way she is I wanted to do two different dinners."

"That's kind of a pain, isn't it?"

"Yeah, it is, but my mom is a pain and I don't want Carter's parents uncomfortable because she says or does something snobby. I don't know how well his parents get along with her since the divorce. I need to have a conversation with my father."

"About what?" she questions as we pull up to the salon.

"What really happened between them? I think it's time I know why my parents divorced and haven't spoken much since. Think about it, he goes to her fundraisers as the owner of several large auto dealerships, but they barely say two words to each other."

"Maybe they said all they needed to say to each other during the divorce."

***

An hour and a half later, I step out of the stylist's chair with some new highlights and a great haircut that is styled and ready for my pictures. I love what my hairdresser did. She added a lot of layers, giving my hair some great body. The front is cut to the shape of my face so that when I blow it out, it sits nicely around my chin. She even showed me how to curl it away from my face if I choose.

When I step around the corner Bella gushes, "You look great! I love what she did with it." She jumps up to hug me. "This is perfect. It's still nice and long for your man, but it has some style to it too, and it really suits you."

My hairdresser says, "I'm glad you both like it. I'll see you ladies before the fundraiser for your hairstyles."

"Thanks," I reply.

Now we're off to our next stop, Kelly's studio, for a round of pictures. It doesn't take us long to get there and when we pull up there's a spot right out front. We park and go inside to see what she has in mind for me.

I'm wearing a dark pair of jeans and a light gray sweater, white boot socks, and black calf-high boots. When Kelly sees me, she's all excited because what I'm wearing goes well with what she had in mind for her backdrop.

"You are going to look great with this backdrop," she says. "Come see." She pulls us into another room where she has it all set up. "I'm going to do a bunch of poses for you and I'll send them to you in color and black and white so you can use what you want."

She has me pose in a few standing positions, first leaning on props and such, and then she puts me on a stool, taking a few more pictures. It takes her about an hour between posing me, changing props and backgrounds, and making sure she's happy with what she sees on the screen of her digital camera.

She finally tells us that she thinks she has plenty and that I'll have some samples to look over this evening. I let her know that I'll give her a shout out in my next book where the picture will appear. We all hug and say our good-byes then Bella and I are off.

"Where do you want to do lunch?" I ask Bella as we walk out to her car.

"Someplace I can eat somewhat healthy because I have another shoot next week and I don't want to put on any weight."

"Oh, I know because you're getting so fat. You better watch out." I shake my head because she's constantly stressing and she's so skinny.

"Yeah, well if I ate half the shit you do, I wouldn't stay this way."

I shrug. "Okay, well wherever you want to go."

"We'll go to that place near the mall that has all the yummy salads."

"The Café?"

"Yeah, that little café," she says, glancing at me.

"No, Bella, it's called The Café."

She chuckles as she pulls up in front of it and sees the sign above the door that says *'The Café.* The place is pretty busy. We get in line to order our food. I decide to have the Fuji salad that has dried apples, chicken, and walnuts. Bella decides on some tofu salad that sounds disgusting. As we're waiting for our food, some girl comes up to me and she's staring at me like I have ten heads.

"Can I help you?" I ask, giving her a look because she's freaking me out.

"Oh my God. You're P.A. Fitzgerald." She's acting totally awestruck, like I'm a movie star.

"Shh, yes I am." I try to get her to lower her voice because I don't want her causing a scene in the café. I've never been approached like this before, and I don't really know what to do. The reporters love me at events, but I feel like it's more because of my mother than my professional status.

"I'm sorry, I'm just so excited. I love all of your books and I'm on your fan page. May I please have your autograph?" She starts digging through her purse for something for me to write on, but I save her the trouble.

"Here." I go into my purse, retrieve one of my bookmarks with all my books listed on it, and scribble my autograph on the back.

"Oh my God! Thank you so much. I can't believe I'm going to say this but my friends will never believe I met you. Can I get a picture and I promise to leave you alone?"

I smile because I don't know what else to do. She's so excited to meet me and it's quite thrilling.

"Sure, hand Bella your phone and she can take the picture."

"Oh it's *you*! You're Bella Campbell the supermodel!" She hands Bella her phone and then jumps up and down like she just won a ton of money. She stands next to me and I wrap my arm around her and she does the same to me. We smile while Bella snaps the picture. The girl thanks me as our number is being called and runs off, I'm certain to post that picture to her Facebook page.

"Look at you! The famous P. A. Fitzgerald takes a picture with a fan in The Café," Bella teases.

We walk off with our salads to find a table in a corner somewhere, and end up finding a seat in the back of the café in a nice quiet area. As soon as we sit down my phone rings.

"Hey, Joan, what's up?"

"I have your contract approved for the eight months with five signings, but I want to be clear the signing you just did doesn't count."

"How do you know about the signing already?" I ask.

"You're flagged every time someone tags you on

Facebook and I get an email alert."

"Joan, that's a little creepy."

"It's my job to know what you're up to and how you're behaving. By the way you handled that well, but be careful because if you're starting to be recognized more in public you'll begin to see more of that."

"I will. Can you just send me the contract? I'm trying to enjoy lunch with Bella and I keep getting interrupted."

"Get used to it. You're *P.A. Fitzgerald,* writer and daughter of Sandra Fitzgerald-Carmichael. It comes with the territory."

"What was that all about?" Bella questions with a concerned look when I end the call.

"My agent gets an email every time someone tags me on Facebook. I told her I thought it was creepy, but she says it's her job to know what I'm doing at all times. I'm not sure how I feel about this."

"I agree with you. I think it's a tad creepy that she's stalking you that closely. I would look into that with some of your other friends who use agents."

"Most of my friends self-publish and if I question it on Facebook she'll see. I may have to call another agency on the down low and see what they say."

"Great. Now you not only have fans stalking you, but an agent too." She chuckles wryly.

"That's not even funny." I look up to see Ben staring at me from across the room. I nod in his direction. She turns to see him and gives him the evil eye. He walks away. "He's another one that creeps me out."

"I don't blame you. He's such an ass and I can't believe he tried to talk to you at the fundraiser like you guys have anything to say after all this time apart."

"I have no doubt that my mother had something to do with that."

Bella gives me a look. "You think she's still on that?"

"Oh, I know she is. That's why I finally had to give it to her straight. She didn't even deny it."

Once we're done with our salads, we leave the table to throw our stuff out and get rid of our tray. On our way out the door I hear someone call my name.

I turn to see it's Ben. I shake my head and keep walking because he will not get any more of my attention.

Our next stop is our favorite boutique just outside the mall. The shopkeeper has the cutest sweaters, tunics, and dresses. We walk in and start going through all the clothes she has hanging. I find one pair of leggings, a matching tunic, and a skirt. As I'm making my purchases my phone rings and it's Carter.

"Hi, honey," I say into the phone.

"Are you still out with Bella?"

I look over at her with a smile. "Yeah, we've had a busy day, but I'm finishing up at the boutique now and then I'm going home to relax a bit and do some posting on my social media pages. Apparently a girl I met today posted a picture I took with her on

Facebook."

"How do you know?"

"My agent called me telling me she saw it. Anyway, I'm going to get going so I can get out of here, but I'll see you in the morning at your new place."

"Yeah, I'm going to meet you there, then I have to run to work. I had the Wi-Fi turned on so you'll have internet access while you work."

"Great, thanks. See you in the morning."

"Have a good night, sweetie."

When I'm done with my call Bella's finishing up with her purchases.

"Are you ready to head home or is there somewhere else you want to go?" she asks.

"I think I'm going to call it a day. I need to call my mother about dinner and do some research for my book. I also want look at what this girl posted and see if I can manage to get some insight about my agent stalking me."

As soon as I'm in the house I dial my mother's number because I want to get this conversation done and over with.

She picks up right away and I can hear in her voice that she's excited. "Hello, darling, how are you?"

"I'm fine, Mother. How are you?"

"I'm so happy to hear from you. What are you up to?"

"I just had lunch with Bella and I was talking to her about getting together for dinner with you, her, and Carter's friend, Derek, at his new apartment. We wanted to have everyone over."

She sighs into the phone. "Are you still seeing that boy?"

"Mother, he is a man not a boy. Please give him a chance. I really like him and he really likes me."

She says nothing for a minute then, "Fine, I will have dinner with you. Text me the address and the time and I'll be there.

"Mother, I don't understand the problem. His family is friends with Dad. They are in a good place and the man has served our country. He may not be as rich as Ben, but not everything in life revolves around money. You should care more about how he treats me than how much money he has."

"I hope he does treat you well, although just because you're happy about dating him doesn't mean I have to be. I said I would be there and that I will give him a chance."

This time I sigh. "I'll text you the info," I say and end the call.

Patty: I just spoke to my mother about dinner.

Carter: How'd it go?

Patty: I'm sorry to say she isn't happy about us dating. I'm nervous about how it's going to go.

Carter: It'll be fine, just relax.

Patty: I hope you're right. I have to go now and get some stuff done. Talk to you soon.

Carter: Good night, sweetie.

Patty: Good night, Carter.

Chapter 14

Patty

With my laptop and overnight bag in hand, I set off for Carter's new apartment. Today is moving day. The furniture is coming and he's supposed to have all of his clothes and the towels his mother bought him at the house. I ran out last night and picked up laundry soap, fabric softener, dishwasher soap, and some small food items. This way I can wash all of his towels while I'm waiting for the furniture to arrive.

I pull up to his building and park in one of his reserved spots. He has two of them and there are plenty of visitor's parking spaces as well. I put my laptop bag over my shoulder then gather the rest of the bags. They're kind of heavy, but when I get to the door, the doorman takes some stuff from me and has someone from the staff help me bring it up. When I get up there, Carter is waiting for me inside. He takes the bags from the staff person and thanks him for helping me bring my stuff up.

"Hey, sweetie," Carter says when we're alone, "What's all of this?"

"My laptop and overnight bag, and since we haven't gone shopping there's no food in the house. I went to get some snacks for me to have while I wait."

"You're planning on drinking laundry soap and fabric softener?"

"Don't knock it until you try it," I say jokingly. "I figured I'd wash the towels and sheets while I waited for the furniture. That way they're clean when it's time for us to make the bed later."

"You are the best," he says as he pulls me in close for a kiss. "I have to go. Thank you so much for waiting here. I've spoken to Derek and he said I can leave early. I'll be home as soon as I can, then we'll go shopping and relax tonight."

"I think we should get things put away and cleaned up tonight then shop in the morning. We can order some Chinese food tonight."

"That's fine too. I'll see you in a few hours." He kisses me again and then he's out the door.

I take a deep breath as I see all the bags around the house. The pans I bought him are still in the box, along with the dishes, cups and utensils. First things first, I need to go wash the towels. I put the laundry detergent and fabric softener away in the laundry room then go in search of the bag with the towels in it. Christ, his mom bought half a store worth of towels. I take the bags to the laundry area to get the first load going. By the looks of it, I've got at least three loads of towels to wash before I do the sheets.

Next I head into the kitchen to put the dishes that I bought him in the dishwasher. I add the utensils and as many glasses as I can fit, put the soap in, and press the start button. Once that's done, I break down the cardboard boxes and open the pans, placing them on the counter, then break down that box as well. I realize we don't have trash bags here. I run to the other room for one of the big shopping bags that the towels were in to use for trash. I put as much cardboard in the bag as I can fit and set it aside. Since I've got the laundry and dishes going, I unwrap the sheets and set them by the washer so I can use the bag for more trash as needed.

Time for a breather. I sit at the snack bar to get started on some work. I log onto my Facebook fan page to see that there are a ton of comments on this girl's picture of us. Of course she even tells them where she saw me. Don't get me wrong, I'm glad I made her day, but she told them one of my hangouts. That'll be great for business at The Café, but not so great for me. I like the food there and now I won't be able to go there for a while because it'll be swamped with local fans. I post a brief write up about how nice it was to meet her and that it makes me so happy to hear that she really enjoys my books.

Opening my email I find Joan's with my new contract. I need to comb through that once I can print it out and really read it over. For now, I scan it for the important parts that I wanted to have listed in it. As promised, Joan added a section that says I'm to get eight months of uninterrupted time off after the final signing is done and all book signings are to be completed within three months of the release of the book. I'm still not sure why I even needed to add this to my contract, but if I find out this agent is being creepy this will be my last contract with her and I'll have to make some decisions before I write my next book.

By the time I'm done looking at Facebook, reading my email, and skimming the contract, the washer is just about done. I stop what I'm doing to go put the first load in the dryer and get another load washing.

After that I get to work on reading what I've written from the last few chapters of my book. As usual, I'm finding mistakes and changing things a bit as I read through it again for a second time. I'm finally at the point where I'll send this off to my beta readers to see what they think about the beginning of the book. I always tell them I will send it to them when the book is complete, but I never do. I've come to realize I like their input as I go. I'm about to click save on my file when the phone rings. It's the doorman telling me the furniture guys are here and he's sending them up with one of the staff.

There are four of them and they tell me that they're going to start with the bedroom set first. While they head back down to start getting pieces, I send Carter a text.

Patty: Furniture is just arriving.

Carter: Great! I'll be getting out of here in a little bit.

Patty: Take your time.

I start on emptying the dishwasher because I have more dishes to run through it, as well as glasses. As I'm finishing putting the clean ones away, the delivery guys come up with the first pieces of furniture. I walk them into his room and tell them where to put it as well as the other pieces.

My phone rings again.

"Hey, Bella," I answer.

"How's the furniture move going?" she asks, sounding out of breath.

"It's going. The furniture guys are here now and I've been washing dishes and towels between working. What are you up to?" She laughs. "Visiting my friend. Can you tell doorman to let me up? I have lunch for you."

The guys are coming back up with Carter's bed and box spring when I walk out of the kitchen.

"What, you're here?"

"Yeah, I came to help you and bring you lunch."

I hang up on her and call down to tell the doorman she's welcome up. While I wait for her, I start folding all the towels from the dryer, moving them to the appropriate bathroom. I put the ones from the wash into the dryer so I can put the sheets washing next.

Bella gets up to the apartment and when she walks in her eyes are wide, "Wow, this is a pretty nice place," she says, looking around. She holds up a bag. "Sandwich?"

"Sure." I open it up on the counter and take a bite while I wait for the guys to finish putting his bed together. "I wish I would've known you were coming, I would've asked you to bring me something to clean these pans with. There are no sponges or dish soap. I only brought dishwashing soap."

"Sorry I wanted to surprise you."

"I'll text Carter."

Patty: Can you pick up sponges and dish soap?

Carter: Sure, why?

Patty: Can't clean the pans without it!

Carter: You're supposed to be working.

Patty: I am ;-)

***

By the time Carter walks in the door, we've managed to wash all the towels, make the bed, do all the dishes, and put them away. We also wiped down all the furniture so it's dust free. He looks around. "My place looks outstanding."

I'm so happy he likes it. "Are you sure you're okay with where I had them put everything? We didn't really discuss it so I just kind of guessed."

"It's perfect, thank you so much."

"Bella, helped," I say as she comes around the corner.

"Hi, I've heard a lot about you. Congrats on your place. It's really nice."

"Thanks, and thanks for being here with Patty to make sure everything was set."

She smiles. "No problem. Listen, I know you two have plans for tonight so I'm going to go. We're on for dinner in a few weeks, so I'll see you again soon."

"Wait, let me at least feed you. I mean, you did all this work with Patty. We can't just let you leave."

He looks at me and I'm so happy because he really is a sweet guy.

"Besides, Derek is on his way over to help me figure out the TV system we picked out. We'll order some Chinese food on me as a thank you for your help."

Bella looks at me, I shrug. "What the heck, I'll stay."

A few minutes later the phone rings and it's the doorman telling us Derek has arrived. We tell him to send him up. I ask if they have Chinese food menus they can send up with him and they tell me no problem. When Derek knocks on the door, Carter lets him in he says, "Chinese food menu delivery man and TV expert on deck."

We all laugh and Carter introduces everyone. I notice Derek instantly checks Bella out and it makes me smile because she's single and it'd be kind of cool for her to date Carter's friend.

The guys get to work on the TV, DVD, and surround sound system while Bella and I order Chinese food. The guys are finishing up as the Chinese food arrives, and we all sit around eating and chatting. Derek learns about Bella being a model and she tells him that she'll be at the next fundraising event even though she's lost her date to a man. He has a scared look on his face until she informs him that *I* was her date.

He laughs. I'm willing to bet they'll be exchanging phone numbers before they leave tonight.

"Thanks to both of you for helping out today," Carter says to Derek and Bella. He turns to me. "I'll thank you properly once they leave."

Derek jumps up. "On that note, I think it's time to go. It was nice to finally meet you, Patty."

"It was nice to meet you too, Derek."

Bella and Derek walk out together, and Carter shuts and locks the door behind them. We walk into his bedroom and when I turn to see his reaction he has another huge smile on his face.

"Thank you again." I wrap my arms around his waist and squeeze him, placing my head on his chest. He wraps his arms around me and kisses the top of my head. "I'm sure you're tired but I'd really like to make love to you tonight."

I smile against his chest because I noticed he used the 'L' word.

"I would really like that."

He places his finger under my chin, lifting it so I look him in the eyes. He lowers his lips and gently presses them to mine. After a moment, he pokes his tongue out, caressing my lips with it before I open to him. Our tongues meet and his hand goes to my nape and we deepen our kiss. I can already feel moisture building below and he's only just started kissing me. He rubs up my back under my shirt, sending goosebumps spreading across my body. His lips leave mine to trail kisses to my ear. He nibbles on my earlobe, his hands roaming over my bare skin. As he kisses his way down my neck, his hands make their way up my back to my bra, unhooking it and freeing my breasts.

"I love the way you smell and taste."

He pulls my shirt over my head. I pull his shirt off at the same time because I want to feel my bare chest pressed to his. I press my lips to his chest and slowly lick and kiss my way toward his collarbone and up his neck. He moans, picking me up and carrying me the rest of the way to the bed. I hold on to his neck while he uses one hand to pull down the sheets before he lays me down. He kicks off his shoes and khakis, slipping in bed beside me.

"I think it's time for dessert," he whispers in my ear. He glides his hand up my leg over my hip, to my belly, and then up to my breast. He's watching as my body reacts to his touch and a smile spreads across his face when he sees my nipples harden even more for him.

He lowers his lips to my nipple, suckling it in while his fingers continue to play with the other one. I moan in pleasure. He kisses across my cleavage to the other breast, paying that one a bit of attention before he licks and kisses his way straight down the middle of my body to the top of my leggings. He's biting, licking, and kissing my hips as he lowers them. I help him get them off, because I'm getting impatient wanting to feel his lips on more of me.

He tosses them to the side and goes back to

kissing and rubbing my legs, but he must be getting impatient too because suddenly his lips are on me. I shudder as his tongue finds my clit and he starts to lick it.

"Oh, Carter," I moan because I love the way his mouth feels on me. He starts sucking on it and it nearly sends me over, but he senses it so he stops and sticks his tongue deep inside me, fucking me with it. As I'm getting close he again stops. "Carter, please don't tease me."

"What's wrong? Do you want to come all over my tongue?"

I groan because I love that he can talk so dirty and I just nod in response.

"Say it, sweetie, tell me what you want."

"Carter," I pause for a second, "Carter, I want to come all over your tongue."

He smiles up at me and starts liking my clit hard and fast. I'm so wound up that in a matter of minutes I'm already close again. I start grinding my hips against his face, but he puts his hands on my hips to hold me still. His tongue slips back into my pussy and his thumb goes to my clit, rubbing it as I explode all over his tongue. God, I love when he does that.

"Carter, yes! I'm coming."

He moans against my pussy as he laps up my juices. He gets up for a condom but I stop him, wanting to taste him.

"It's getting late," he says, "and I need to be buried deep inside of you. Please let me."

I bite my lip and nod shyly because I love that he loves my pussy so much. He leans down to kiss me gently, gets a condom, and rolls it into place.

"I hope you're ready for me because I really want to feel you."

"I'm ready."

He lines himself up and slams himself deep inside of me. He slowly picks up the pace, ensuring I feel the full length of his huge cock gliding in and out of me. We fit so well together.

"Carter, please give me more," I beg.

He starts pumping himself into me harder and faster. I wrap my legs around his hips changing the angle slightly as he continues to slam into me.

"Patty, I can't hold on much longer and I want to feel you milking my cock." A second later I'm screaming his name as another orgasm tears through me, shaking my body as I milk him for all he has.

"Damn, woman, I think you're trying to kill me. I thought I was going to have to stop for a minute."

He pants on top of me, pressing me into his new mattress with his warm, strong body. "I love how you feel on top of me like this."

He looks down at me with a smile. "That's funny because this is my favorite place for you."

He slips himself out of me to get rid of the condom. He comes back and slides into bed behind me, wrapping his arm around me, and we both fall asleep.

***

I'm half asleep when I realize I'm hearing something. It's grunting and groaning, and I realize it's Carter. I lay in his bed listening to him mumble in his sleep, unsure if I should wake him or not. I didn't know he had nightmares like this and I don't recall hearing him have one at my house. He has such a pained look on his face, I decide to wake him from it because it's killing me to see him this way. He looks so upset and is soaked in sweat. I reach over and gently shake him.

"Carter, it's Patty, wake up. You're having a nightmare." The gentle motion does nothing to bring him out of it. I shake him a bit harder, but when I do he jumps up, covers my mouth, and pins me to the bed.

"Who are you and what do you want?" He has pure rage in his eyes and I'm scared. I don't know what to do. He has no idea who I am, and I have no idea if he's still sleeping. I lay there completely still, afraid if I move he'll think I'm trying to hurt him.

Suddenly he snaps out of it. "Oh my God, Patty, I'm so sorry. Did I hurt you?" He climbs off me, letting me up.

I climb out of bed a bit shaken for a minute. "What the hell was that all about, Carter?"

He sighs and sits on the side of the bed. "I'm sorry. I should have warned you, but I didn't know how to bring it up. I have nightmares. It wasn't an issue because I haven't been in a relationship since I've been home, and I had no idea I would react that way. I was afraid I'd wake you but I didn't know I would pin you like that, I'm so sorry."

"Have you spoken to anyone about it?"

"Only Derek. I tried going to counseling, but they had no idea what it's like. The things we go through can't be understood unless you're there. They act like they get it just because they've heard stories and studied books."

I climb back in bed to hold him, "I'm sorry you had to go through that. We need to figure something out because you scared the shit out of me."

"I know, and I'm so sorry. Derek told me I should bring it up to you and he thinks that is part of the reason I have them. I am internally stressing over the fact that I hadn't told you. Maybe now that you know, they'll go away."

"You have to promise me that if they don't you'll get help, Carter."

He nods. "I promise. If the nightmares continue now that you know I'll get help. Just please be patient with me."

"Come on, snuggle me so we can try to get a little more sleep before we have to get up and start our busy day."

He spoons me from behind, pulling me close, kisses the top of my head, and says, "I'm so sorry, Patty."

I take his hand, giving him a squeeze to let him know it will be okay, and I drift back off to sleep.

Chapter 15

Carter

I've spent most of the night watching Patty sleep. I feel so bad that I attacked her in my sleep. I only remember bits and pieces of the dream. I remember being on patrol when suddenly someone grabbed me. I think that's why I pinned Patty down. I felt like I was being attacked. Although I don't want to admit it to her, I'm afraid to go back to sleep because I don't want to hurt her or scare her again. I'm going to have to talk to Derek or someone who's been in my shoes about ways to have her wake me if I'm having a nightmare. I keep dozing off for short periods of time but when I start to feel myself going into a deep sleep I wake up again. I can't seem to shut my mind off enough for me to sleep peacefully and I know it's because I'm worried about her. I love having her in my bed, but I would never forgive myself if I ever hurt her.

I finally doze off, dreaming about Patty and her hot body until I wake at about seven-thirty in the morning, this time with a massive hard-on. I decide it's time to wake my princess for some morning loving. She's lying beside me fully naked and it makes me smile. I glide my hand up her leg, stopping at her sweet pussy. I gently press my fingers through her folds, discovering that she's already wet for me. It makes me wonder if she was dreaming about me. I lower my lips to her nipple and gently suck it into my mouth. I roll my tongue over it and she moans slightly as it hardens in my mouth. I gently slide two fingers into her now fully soaked pussy. I curl my fingers inside of her, working her up to an orgasm.

I'm not sure she's even awake yet until she says, "Good morning to you too." I continue curling my fingers deep inside her. "My God, Carter, you're going to make me come."

"That's my plan, sweetie." I continue to finger fuck her with one hand and I use my other to massage her clit. Her hips start moving in rhythm with my fingers and just when she's about to explode, I stop.

"Carter, what are you doing?" She's panting, upset that I'm making her wait.

"What's wrong, sweetie, were you about to come?"

"Um, yeah," she says, totally frustrated.

I start pumping my fingers in and out of her again, but this time I lower my mouth to massage her clit with my tongue. She's so worked up she explodes all over my fingers as I lick her clit. I can feel her insides tightening around me as she screams my name and rides it out.

She rolls over on top of me and lowers her mouth to mine in a passionate kiss. She breaks it to kiss her way to my ear, and whispers, "I'm going to ride you. I hope you're ready." She then lifts herself so she can slide my length deep inside her. She lifts her ass and slams back down on top of me. I grab her hips and start meeting her thrust for thrust. God she feels so good.

"Carter, I'm going to come again."

"Give it to me, sweetie." I slam into her one more time and she does just that. Her muscles tighten around me and I find my release. Only after we finish I realize we didn't use a condom.

"Shit, Patty, we were so in the moment, we didn't use a condom."

She collapses on top of me telling me that she's on the pill and that's the first time she's ever done it without a condom. I tell her it is for me too and that I can show her all my medical records if she wants. She smiles down at me, "I trust you, Carter, but we should still probably be careful just in case."

"I agree, but damn that felt good. You have the sweetest pussy I've ever had."

She giggles and buries her face in my chest. I roll her over and tell her I'm not done yet. I start kissing her and we begin round two.

I finally let her out of bed so we can clean up and get something to eat before we run around for the day. Thanks to the food she picked up yesterday, we have muffins for breakfast. I have absolutely no food in this house. Patty comes into the kitchen dressed and ready to go. I lean in to give her a kiss before I pull out her chair. Removing a piece of paper from her laptop bag she says, "So what do you want to stock in this place?"

"Food."

"Funny, Carter. What would you like for food?"

"You know, the basics, bread, cereal, milk, soup, eggs." I bite into my muffin.

She rolls her eyes. "This is going to be fun."

I shrug. "Write what you need for tonight and we'll decide on everything else while we are there."

I can already tell she likes order in her life and not having a list does not show order. I'm the same way with many things but not having a grocery list doesn't bother me.

"It'll be fine."

She nods and continues making a list for tonight. "I know what I need for tonight, but you don't have a roasting pan that's big enough so I need to pick one up while we're out."

"No problem. We'll go to that huge grocery store up the street that sells everything. They're a bit more expensive, but it'll be worth it to only make one stop." She taps the pen on the counter like she's debating something, but of course, I have no idea what's going on in that pretty head of hers. "Talk to me, Patty."

"I guess I'm just a little nervous about tonight. I want things to be perfect for our parents. It's our first dinner with us all together. Our parents have been friends for years, what if they kept us apart for a reason and this all blows up in our face?"

"Sweetie, slow down. I've spoken to my parents and they've made no mention about being upset or having a problem with us being together. Has your father?"

She shakes her head. "I guess I'm just scared because I'm starting to really like you and dealing with my mom is enough. I want my dad's support, you know?"

"I get it, and I promise to be on my best behavior." I try to give her a playful smile to lighten the mood. I bump her and she looks up at me trying to fight her smile but she's failing miserably.

"Let's get the groceries over with so we can come home and I can make love to you in the shower before they get here."

She shakes her head. "You're insatiable."

"Only when it comes to you." I kiss her on the forehead.

She climbs off the stool and heads over to the coat closet to get her jacket. On the way out I let the doorman know that we'll be back shortly. He opens the door for us and says, "Have a good day."

***

We arrive back to my apartment two hours later with what feels like endless bags of food. We have bought everything from breakfast food, to meat for the freezer, and lunch meat for the fridge. This wonderful woman of mine has made sure I have everything I need to make healthy lunches and make easy stuff for myself if she isn't here giving me cooking lessons.

Trying to decide where everything is going to go was a bit harder than I thought. We get everything put away and cleaned up in time for us to relax a bit before our parents come over this evening. I love the take charge attitude that comes from this five foot seven woman with a big heart. As she's putting the milk, beer, and wine in the fridge, I can't help but place my hand on her sweet little ass.

"Carter," she says, pretending to be frustrated.

When she turns around, I close the door to the fridge, pinning her against it. "What, sweetie?" Before she can answer I lower my lips to hers and she moans into my mouth. I pull away, resting my forehead against hers. "Thank you again for all of your help."

She grins up at me. "You're so welcome."

Rubbing my hands up the sides of her body, I lower my lips to her ear and whisper, "I need to feel you under me one more time before we deal with our parents." She sucks in a breath in as I gently bite her earlobe and then kiss down her neck to her collarbone. "Please tell me I can have you one more time."

She moans as my hand slides under her shirt and squeezes her nipple. She grabs my hand and tugs me off in the direction of my room.

"I'll take that as a yes."

I scoop her up and carry her to the side of my bed. When I place her down in the middle I kick my shoes off and lay on top of her, looking straight into her eyes and thinking about how scared I am that I care for her so much in such a short period of time. I'm afraid to tell her so I decide to show her. I pour all of my feelings into this kiss, hoping she realizes what I feel for her. When I break the kiss to look into her eyes again, she smiles at me and in that moment I feel like she knows just how I feel.

I lift her shirt and pull her breasts from the cups of her bra so I can suck her tiny pink nipples into my mouth, listening for that sensuous moan I love, and she doesn't disappoint. I glide my tongue slowly down the center of her flat belly over her belly button to the top of her leggings. I peel them down her body and she lifts her ass to help me get them off. Once I have them off I lick and kiss my way back up her leg until I reach her pussy, then I kiss my way back down the other leg just to be a tease.

She growls, letting me know she's not happy and I can't help but chuckle. "Want something?"

"Yes, please," she says in the sweetest voice she can muster.

I strip off my jeans and boxers, climbing up her body and sticking only the tip of my cock inside her while looking into her eyes. "Is this what you want?"

She smiles and nods, trying to move her hips so I'll go deeper inside her. I slowly start sliding my cock deeper and deeper until she's taken my full length. Her eyes close in pleasure. I gradually pick up the pace and when I know she's getting close I tell her to open them for me.

Once she's looking into my eyes I start slamming my cock deeper into her so she'll give me what I want.

"Carter," she moans, fighting not to close her eyes.

"Give me what I want," I growl and she does, her orgasm shaking her entire body. Her pussy tightens around my cock, sucking every last drop of my seed from me.

***

I find Patty in the kitchen going to town chopping onions and getting the pork ready to go into the oven.

"How can I help, sweetie?"

She looks up at me with the sweetest smile. "Can you peel potatoes for me?"

"I can do that." I get the peeler as well as the potatoes we picked up from the store today and get to work.

I notice we are silent as we're doing our thing in the kitchen. It's quiet, but it's a comfortable silence. We move well together as we work around each other getting things done. I'm about halfway through the potatoes when I decide we need to try my new surround sound system.

"Would you like a little music?" I ask her and she simply nods as she's placing a piece of meat in the pan. After the click of a few buttons we have soft music playing all around us. I go back to finish the potatoes because I know she's almost ready for them and just as I'm doing the last one she's rinsing them and placing them in the pan.

"Just so you know, student," she says to me in a teasing tone, "all I've done is put meat, potatoes, onion, and asparagus in a pan."

"What's next, my sexy cooking teacher?"

"I bought this packet of seasoning. We need your big measuring cup and you're going to add the oil and water, then we add this packet, mix it with a fork, and pour it over the top. That's it."

"Really, it's that easy?"

"Somewhat. You have to make sure you don't overcook it because if you do your pork is going to be dry and that'll suck. We'll set a timer and we bought a thermometer, so we'll be fine."

"Maybe I should try getting some cookbooks. I've never tried doing that before."

She shrugs. "I can look for some for you," she says, opening the oven door and sliding in the foil covered roasting pan.

"Just the Way You Are" by Bruno Mars comes on and I walk over to her, taking her hand and pulling her into my arms. She wraps her arms around my waist and I start swaying with her to the music, looking into her eyes.

Although I can't sing too well, I whisper some of the words to her. I want her to know how beautiful I think she is. She blushes and looks at the floor.

"Don't look down, beautiful."

"I'm sorry, I've just never had anyone talk to me or treat me the way you do. You look at me and see more than the plain, boring book nerd I've always been."

She looks down again, embarrassed to call herself a book nerd, but I take her chin and lift it so she's forced to look into my eyes. "There's nothing plain or boring about you and I'm sorry that no one has ever shown you how beautiful, smart, and sexy you are."

She sighs. "I guess I just hadn't found the right man. I was with Ben for almost a year, but he cared more about how he looked in public then our relationship. I tried so hard to care about him, but he was such a jerk. I slept with him hoping it would bring us closer together, but he never cared about my feelings or taking care of me. It was always about him and his needs. I finally realized that I was with him more for my mother than myself. When he snapped and hit me, that was my out and I took it."

I hug her tenderly. "Patty, I know when I jumped on you in bed last night it must have scared you and I didn't mean to. Please know I'll never hurt you intentionally like that."

She places her hand on my cheek. "I know, and you're right, you scared me, but as long as you're working on it I'm okay with that."

"Good. Will you spend the night with me again tonight?"

"Absolutely."

I scoop her up and spin her around in my kitchen. She giggles at my playfulness and it's the most beautiful sound in the world.

"You make me so happy," I tell her as I set her back down on the floor.

"I'm glad, but I need to go change now that dinner's in the oven.

***

The phone rings. It's the doorman telling me that my guests are on their way up.

I look at Patty. "Ready?"

She nods and there's a knock on the door. We walk over together to answer it and both my parents and her father are here for our night together. My mom hugs me, gushing over how grown up Patty is and how it's been ages since she's seen her. We welcome them in and I show them around while Patty pours wine and beers.

"Darling, I'm so proud of you," my mom says. "You have picked a lovely place and you did an excellent job selecting things to put in it."

"Mom, I owe a lot of it to Patty. I may have found the place but she helped me pick everything inside of it." I place my arm around her neck. "She also stayed here while I was at work to be sure the delivery guys got everything here and in place."

"You sweet girl," my mother says. "Thank you so much for helping our son."

"It's really not a problem. I can write from anywhere."

"Yeah, Mom, she says that, but she didn't even write. She washed all my towels and my sheets so they would be fresh for my bed. She's amazing."

"That's my girl," her father says, kissing her on the head. "Your mother would have had a cleaning crew in here, but not you. You've never been afraid to get your hands dirty. I'm proud of you, baby girl."

Poor Patty is blushing from her head to her toes.

"Thanks, Daddy. You're lucky I could never stay mad at you long. Mr. 'I don't listen and send someone to watch over my daughter anyway.'" I give my father a look and he and Patty's dad start laughing.

"What are you talking about?" he asks, playing innocent. "Really, Daddy? You're still going to go with the 'I don't know what you're talking about line?'" She's pretending to be mad and failing miserably.

"Baby girl, you're my daughter and I will always protect you. If that means being on your shit list for a few days, I'm okay with that." He hugs her again and she laughs.

"Sorry, sir," I say, "she beat it out of me."

Her father grins. "I'm sure it didn't take much. Patty has a way with people. She can make them talk pretty easily."

"So, Patty, what is this new book you're working on?" my mom asks her.

Patty starts to tell my parents all about her new book and how she's hoping to be done by the end of January so she can have some of the summer off.

The timer goes off on the oven and Patty excuses herself to check on dinner. I decide to join her to see if she needs help. She opens the oven door and a delicious aroma comes bursting from the oven and suddenly I'm starving. I hand her the meat thermometer so she can check the internal temp. She shows me how the thermometer tells me if the meat is ready or not making, it easier on someone like me who's learning to cook. Once we determine dinner is done we call everyone into the kitchen so we can eat. We already have everything set up on the snack bar since I haven't found a dining set I like yet.

"Carter, are you going to get a dining room set soon?" my mother asks me.

"I'd like to, I'm hoping I can convince Patty to help me cook Thanksgiving dinner and have everyone here."

Patty looks up at me with the biggest smile and I whisper, "I'm sorry, did I put you on the spot?"

"It's okay. I'd love to help you with Thanksgiving dinner."

"Great. Looks like Thanksgiving will be here," I say, handing a plate of food to my mom.

We make the remainder of the plates and I can't believe how excited I am about getting the entire family together.

As I sit down my father says to Patty, "Where's your mother? She couldn't make it?"

Patty visibly tenses. "We're having her over another night. I know there is tension with the three of you so I made it easy for you."

"You guys didn't have to do that," my mom says. "We would have been fine. Patty, your mom and I were friends at one point but we had a disagreement on ways of life. We're both polite in the public eye, but just because we are no longer friends doesn't mean we can't be civil."

"I appreciate that, but we wanted a nice dinner with our parents and she and I are not seeing eye to eye these days. Carter and I decided for our first dinner with the family to keep it separate."

"I understand, and I'm sorry you two are not getting along. I hope you can work it out," my mother says with a sincere voice.

I can see Patty's mood is shifting and I don't want this dinner to go downhill because of a woman that isn't even in the room with us. Just as I'm about to say something my father jumps in.

"On a happier note," he says, "what can we bring

for Thanksgiving?"

"How about a dessert, and we will take care of the main meal?" I turn to Patty. "How does that sound."

"That sounds great," she says sounding genuinely pleased, and I'm not sure anyone else notices but she visibly relaxes at the change in subject. She takes a few more bites of her dinner and pushes her plate away, sipping her wine.

"Let me know if you'd like us to get here early so I can help in the kitchen," my mom offers. "I love to cook and I wouldn't mind."

"That would be nice." Patty takes her plate and heads to the other side of the snack bar to start cleaning up. My mom gets up to join her and I hear them talking about her book world and some of the things she has to do to be successful besides writing. Patty is telling her about her book signings and some of the interesting people she's met along the way.

The guys are discussing my new job and my boss. I'm filling them in on some of the training I've done and some of the benefits available to vets that I hadn't known about.

Once the ladies are done cleaning the kitchen Patty's father says, "It's getting late. I think I'm going to head out, but I'll see you at the dinner next weekend and I can't wait to have Thanksgiving here with everyone."

"Okay, Daddy, thanks so much for coming. It was fun." Patty hugs her dad.

"We're going to go too," my father says.

Patty hugs my parents and her father one more

time. We thank them again for coming and when we're about to close the door, her father turns to me and says, "My daughter has been through enough with her mother and her ex. She may not realize it but I heard what happened at the fundraiser. I don't trust that guy and I have a feeling he isn't going to walk away that easily. Make sure you take good care of my baby girl."

I smile at him confidently. "Sir, trust me when I say I plan on it."

To be continued with *My Broken Soldier-Love Conquers Life 2*

Acknowledgments

I want to give a huge shout out to the ladies of Bonded By Books! As you read in the dedication to book one of this series. My writing began with this group and if it weren't for this group I may have never started. Thanks to them, what was supposed to be a standalone book has turned into a series, Love Conquers Life. Some of you have read for me, some have allowed me to pick your brain and some have promoted for me, no matter what you've done, you're always there for me so thank you, thank you, thank you for all of your love and support!

I also want to give another shout out to my mom. Thanks mom, for all of your love and support. It means the world to me that you not only buy my books but you brag about them to all of your friends. I'm so lucky to have such a supportive mom who drives two days to see her daughter attend her first author signing event. You're the best! I love you to the moon and back.

To my hubby who gets a shout out in every book. I wouldn't be able to do what I do without you. Thank you for working so hard to take care of our family so I can stay home and do what I love. I love you more than words can say. I thank you a million times over for all of your love and support.

About the Author

Alison Mello is a wife and stay at home mom to a wonderful little boy. She lives with her amazing family in Massachusetts. She loves playing soccer, basketball and football with her son.

After having her son, Alison started reading again and fell in love with Contemporary Romance. Reading made her happy and gave her something to do when she had downtime. As she started to read more, she started to noticed things she really enjoyed in a book and things she didn't. She began to have ideas for writing one of her own. One day she literally woke up and started writing. She realized that if there was ever a time for her to write, it was now. She had a part time job to give her something to do. The hours at work were slow and she was bored with what she was doing, so while her son was off enjoying his friends over summer vacation she got started.

Alison finished the first book in two weeks and decided that she really enjoyed writing, so she kept going. She already had ideas in mind for books two and three, so she kept writing. That is how the Learning to Love Series was born. Somewhere along the line, one of my Beta readers convinced me that Michael, a character from Finding Love, needed his own story. That is when Alison added the fourth and final book. Alison hopes you enjoy her books as much as she enjoyed writing them.

She's so glad she started this writing journey and hopes you will stay with her for the ride. Chasing Dreams is scheduled to release in April and the first two books of the Love Conquers Life series will be out this summer!

Facebook:
http://www.facebook.com/alisonmelloauthor

Twitter:
http://www.twitter.com/alisonmelloauth

Website:
http://www.alisonmelloauthor.com/

Goodreads:
http://www.goodreads.com/alisonmelloauthor

Made in the USA
Lexington, KY
08 November 2017